Kimberling Bridge

by

Jeffrey W. Tenney

Whistle Creek Press 2019
ISBN: *978-0-9796333-1-7*
First Edition

for
a Future

Camp Twain Map

As Modified by William

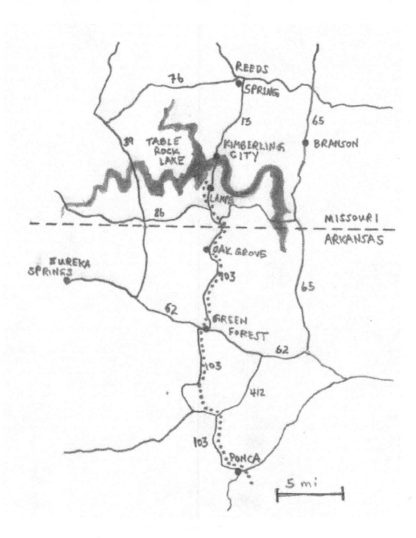

Chapter 1

1

THE BROWN RICE AND BEANS of breakfast tasted like the brown rice and beans of supper, and like every other meal William had eaten over the past three days. Soon as this day was done, he would make his way through the woods again under cover of darkness to his cache, and he would pick out something different this time. That is, if he chose to survive the day. The revolver was now his best friend, the one sure pass to the exit door for an aging life. Survival was not an assumption he cared to make anymore. If he did make such an assumption, he would have to think about what he might do with the time it bought. Avoiding the prospect of time made more sense, either in that final way, or by finding something more to do than lying in his sleeping bag or sitting by his fire with a poker waiting for that something to come to him. Little ever came but empty minute after empty minute. Nothing ever changed but the length of shadows from busted concrete slabs and the tall oaks along the riverbank, and the flow of the water as it slid down out of who knew where to who knew what, like it had some purpose. It had no more purpose than the shadows, no more than he had. No damn reason for anything to be moving at all.

The predawn light sifted through a dense, ultramarine haze that swamped the broken concrete lumps and twisted iron rods of the former bridge. Sitting beneath one of the intact shoreline sections of the bridge, William simply watched as the light slowly paled and thinned, occasionally stirring the small fire that had warmed his breakfast.

He had slept better this past night than on previous nights under this ruin of a bridge. No reason he could think of for that, except perhaps that he was just getting accustomed to it. From his little hideaway, all the world seemed at total peace with itself, and had since his arrival eight days earlier. The rumbles and moans of distant car traffic that had once dominated the nights along this river had not followed him here. Highway 43, County Road 371, County Road 902, which from an aerial view had his house neatly boxed in, had gone stone quiet before he left that house.

It had been the sudden, intense quiet that concerned him most. It meant that normalcy had become a thing now gone for certain. Three months of increasingly worrisome news reports on TV hadn't convinced him. Even when the power went out, when his cell phone died and his truck wouldn't start, there had to be another explanation, something ordinary and reparable. Then came the inexplicable noises from over the hills and the columns of black smoke rising into the downriver sky. But, no, such things were probably there all along, he just hadn't noticed them. But when the Big Quiet came down, the brick that he called his head finally got the message. Home was no cover. Not anymore. The screaming and the shooting and the burning were coming his way, but with silent steps that he would not hear until it was too late.

His first action had been to restart his truck, which he managed to do despite the lack of cooperation from the computerized parts. The second had been to visit the store. He had bought it on his retirement and move down from Minnesota to Arkansas. Same week that he bought the house. The Minnesota state pension and social security were not going to be enough; he needed to squeeze something more out of the local economy, and the little country store at the corner of CR 371 and CR 902 had done that for him.

On his way to the store, he had stopped his pickup well short of what looked like a traffic foul up at the intersection of CR 380 and Hwy 43. Two cars and a van involved. He pulled out his birding binoculars and counted four limp figures being dragged from the van by two quite healthy looking, and well-armed, young men. The van appeared to have been splattered with bullets, the bodies likewise, drenched in blood. He veered off, down a fire lane he had used before, and cut over to Highway 371.

That one trip to the store had been all he could dare. One pickup load of canned and dried foods, batteries, lighters and matches, bullets for his revolver, cordage, camo tarps, and a sizeable stock of further items that would sustain him for…well, for a while.

On the trip home from the store, he had lost about a fourth of his load to sharp turns and urgency, and over-enthusiastic packing—far too much for his old Ford Ranger. He suspected that one of those smoke columns he saw later from the bridge signaled the end for his store.

If what had happened was what he now believed it was, then there would be nothing, no one, capable of stopping the chaos. Political leaders would disappear overnight, probably meeting up with their CEO buddies in some remote but comfortable ocean island, with all the wealth and other goodies their jets could carry. The seven billion other people in the world would be on their own, to live as long as they could off what a ruined economy and all means of production had left for them. The ticking clock had started on the species. Old as he was, he was as young as everyone else, at that point.

2

When William thought about his current situation, beneath that bridge, he had to admit that it differed only in a material way from how things had been before. Like a young fool, he had believed a new start in a new place would mean a new view on life. A house in the country, surrounded by buzzing bees and birdsong in the trees. That was the ticket. He was soon reminded, however, that bad could get worse. By and large, the people he met in the Arkansas woods were the embodiment of the worst, a damn close approximation of the stereotype— undereducated, selfish, short-sighted, intolerant of anything that didn't remind them of themselves, and ultimately self-destructive. They were a stain on the natural beauty he had come for, and were indifferent to it in every way, except as a place to shoot and kill whatever moved among the trees or scurried through the grass. Too bad they had to take the rest of the world down with them. But they did that with seeming ease, with no more trouble than dropping a fox squirrel from a low limb with a 12-gauge. In a flash the whole world went Arkansas. A couple of bizarre elections of the wrong people, with some of the best people looking the other way, and suddenly the hole was too deep to crawl out of, and with everything spiraling downward.

Perhaps if he had retired to Oregon instead, he could have saved the world. But there had been a kind of inevitability to it. The end had been baked into the cake from the beginning. Plenty of historical examples along the way presaged the grand finale. Humans had proved themselves a disgrace to the entire planet.

3

His ninth day under the ruins of the bridge passed as anticipated—quietly. He spent some time trying to divine what sort of motive someone might have to blow up this backroad bridge, a seemingly pointless act in the midst of all the truly significant happenings at the time. But then, there was nothing any one person could do to stop the insanity, which meant this act was not intended for that purpose. He, or they, would have gone to some trouble to acquire the explosives and the know-how for employing them. Was it their intention to target a middle-of-nowhere bridge, or was it merely a target of easy opportunity? Did they have some personal animosity toward this bridge in particular? Were they locals who resented it being built in the first place, who wanted to make a final statement on the matter? Or did someone on one side of the bridge believe that by taking it down he could prevent intruders, violators, from accessing his sanctuary? The river here posed no serious barrier, bridge or no bridge. Sanctuary was a concept so ludicrous that only someone totally deluded could hold it for more than a second. But then, this was Arkansas. And, for him, this bridge was his sanctuary.

Although built on a backroad, and narrow, the bridge had been substantial. It arched a healthy twenty feet at its highpoint as it climbed from the lower bluff on his side to the high bluff on the other. He was no engineer, or government planner, but it seemed a serious case of overspending, given the amount of traffic it had carried.

His house had been no more than six miles upriver from the bridge. He had canoed down to it many times to fish, or just to see what kind of sport the water might have in store for him along the way. In the beginning, he had expected to meet interesting people on the river, urban people looking for some outdoor fun. Many had been urban, but few were interesting. There were none, actually, who were interesting. Nature, indifferent as he knew she was to the minds of people, could at least confirm his opinion of them.

But, goddamn, he had become such a cynic. He hadn't wanted to. It was forced on him. He knew, without a doubt, that it was not in his genes. It was not a case of personal misfortune, either, like having an abusive parent. It was systematically forced on him by the actions of his own species. How else could a reasonable man react to all the bullshit?

When dusk finally fell, he emptied what food remained in the largest of his two backpacks and dug the flashlight out of his small pack. He scraped the last of the rice-and-beans dinner from his pan into his mouth and washed the pan and his fork in the river. The fire was nearly out, so he allowed it to fade into coals while he waited for the deep dark. The fire was well concealed from view in every direction, but the flashes of reflected firelight off the rocks might draw unwanted attention. He cinched his boots up tight and tucked his revolver into his belt. Should have had a holster for it, but he had never expected to need one. The gun had sat uselessly on his closet's high shelf, buried under unused clothing, since the day he moved in.

He was starting to his feet when he heard the "scrunch, scrunch" of pea gravel on the road above and behind him.

Definitely footsteps. Human in their weight and timing. One person. Probably adult male.

William lowered to a squat and held still but for a hand that moved onto his pistol grip. His heart rate quickened.

The footfalls progressed evenly onto the section of the bridge above his head, then slowed before coming to a stop near the edge of the high gap where the explosion had ripped the bridge in half at its peak. William waited.

He couldn't see a damn thing in the dark of the Ozark woods. The quiet was so extreme he worried his breathing might be enough to give him away. Where the hell were the crickets? They always started in about this time, raising a steady buzz out of the woods. He felt his fingers tighten instinctively around the pistol grip.

Suddenly a loud "thud" broke the silence.

It was more than a thud. Something more multidimensional, incorporating various crunching and snapping sounds layered over and about one another. A soft splash followed, as whatever had been tossed, or fallen, off the bridge slipped from the rocks and concrete into the water.

Silence returned just as suddenly, bookending the event.

He waited for the footsteps of retreat, but none came, and he let the moments pass without twitch of muscle or internal remark. Until enough had passed that he grew increasingly certain the event was completed. Nevertheless, he waited it out.

At last the crickets kicked in, followed by a bullfrog's croaking from somewhere in the weeds nearby. He felt the cooling night breeze curling around his collar, and the dryness in his mouth and throat.

The world was coming back from wherever it had hidden itself. Remnants of smoke off his dying fire crawled up into his nostrils. His six-shooter was now in his hand, free of his belt, having decided on its own, he concluded, sometime during the last ten minutes. With his left hand, he dabbed about the darkened ground until he located the flashlight. He gave the whole business another five minutes before deciding he had crossed the line between caution and paranoia. He stood, clicked on the light, and went to investigate.

4

The broad streaks of blood on one of the larger rocks, leading down to the edge of the water, convinced him right away that the plunge had been head-first. Only a head could bleed that much and that fast. The halting of the footsteps at the gap and the delay before the fall marked it a suicide. But no body was in sight.

He scanned the rocks and concrete and water again with his light beam but turned up nothing. The current had carried away the body.

He fumbled his way up and over the rocks and back to his camp, where he laid his gun aside at arm's length, emptied his pockets, and readied his bed of green twigs and grass for another sleep. He started to remove his boots, then decided he had best leave them on this night, in case of further encroachments.

"Screw it," he said to himself out loud as he lay down. "Screw it," again, as he propped his head on his sweat-stained pillow and pulled his sleeping bag around him. He wondered if he had enough rice and beans to hold him for another day. He noticed his heart rate was back to normal. Threat over. An owl some distance off called out while the crickets picked up their chatter. None of *them* gave a shit.

5

In the morning, he found the body trapped in the branches of a young oak overhanging the current about forty yards downstream of his camp. Up to his waist in the clear water of the Buffalo River, he wrangled the body free, then dragged it onto a small gravel bar near the bank. It was a young man, mid to late thirties, dressed in jeans and a tee-shirt. Not someone he recognized from the area. He pulled the man's wallet from his back pocket. James Gordon, it read; thirty-six years old by the birthdate. No cash, only a few pictures—a young girl, a woman about the same age as him, and an older couple—parents, maybe.

In the absence of a pick and shovel, a grave was out of the question given the rocky ground of this part of the country. William simply replaced the wallet and shoved the body back into the current, far enough out that it would carry beyond his sight. Out of sight, out of mind.

Back at his camp, he filled his cooking pot with rice and picked up his one-gallon plastic water jug, now only a third full. He stopped himself before adding the water, lifted the pot to his nose and smelled the rice and felt his throat tighten. He set the pot back down, grabbed and shouldered the empty backpack, and set off.

Chapter 2

1

THE HIKE TO HIS CACHE was only a quarter mile. William wished it were further from the river, to avoid discovery, but then the longer trip for him to and from. As it was, he had to take what was available: a small cave and a spring of fresh water on the bluff, which he had come upon by accident a few years before while looking for arrowheads in the little streambed that ran from the spring to the river. This time of year, late summer, the stream was dry, the spring water disappearing underground no more than a few yards from where it issued from the hillside.

The fresh water, he needed. The cache of food and supplies was even more crucial. The cave opening was a little higher on the bluff than the spring, but only a hundred yards or so. Even so, it was tough to get to through the tight undergrowth of oak saplings, honeysuckle, and wild rose. The cave was invisible from anywhere any sane or even insane person was likely to be, and William did his best to avoid making a trail from the spring, taking a different route each time and using the bare stones for footholds wherever possible.

With a little work moving rocks around inside the cave, he had managed to enlarge it to where it could hold all fifteen of the heavy-duty plastic bins he had lugged in from his canoe. Six canoe trips from his pickup and about thirty overland treks from the river brought in the food and supplies to fill those bins. Two days of solid work that had damn near crippled his back. Each bin was locked, although no lock was going to keep out someone with a degree of determination. The keys, he hid nearby. He had waking nightmares about some of the local undeserving shitheads stumbling upon his cache and living like kings until he came by and shot them. Or they shot him.

With his water bottle refilled and his backpack stuffed with six cans of corn, two of cooked spinach, three of green beans, one of peaches, three of tuna fish, smoked turkey strips, four small bags of brown rice, and more dried black beans, he headed back through the woods to camp. It was a shorter trip back using the river, where a brush pile concealed his canoe, but it was also far too easy to be spotted out there on the water.

2

Back at camp, he saw that his small backpack lay open and not where he had left it, on the opposite side of the fire. He slipped the large pack from his shoulder and reached for his .357 but was stopped short by a high-pitched scream. "I have a gun!"

He looked to his right and saw a small figure step out from behind a pile of concrete slabs, pistol in hand.

A kid. A girl, no more than fourteen. Her hands trembled slightly, but her eyes suggesting she knew what she was doing.

"What is this?" he asked.

Her response came slowly. "Where's my dad?"

"What?"

She raised her voice a notch. "Where's my dad?"

She was about five feet tall, with shoulder-length brown hair and blue eyes, face thin and lightly sunburned.

"I don't know what you're talking about," he said. "Who's your dad?"

She raised her aim from his stomach to his head.

"Hold on there," he said. "I won't answer to a gun. You'll need to put that down."

She hesitated. The gun started down but then came back up. "I ain't joking with you, old man. I'll plumb shoot you through the eye, you don't tell me."

He raised a hand. "Hold on. I believe you. But I can't talk with a girl who's about to murder me."

"Where's my dad, you son of a bitch!"

They stood quietly for a few moments. "You want something to eat?" he said, pointing to his food pack. "I've got all kinds to pick from."

"Shut that! Where's my dad, or I'm gonna blow a hole in you!"

"Good God." He bent forward to set the water jug on the ground, then squatted beside the fire. "Go ahead, then. But I won't be able to tell you anything about your dad if I'm dead."

He stared directly at her and saw the tension build in her face. Her arms seemed to sag slightly under the weight of the gun.

"I have a gun, too," he said, "but I'd never point it at a stranger." After another quiet moment, he added, "Well, maybe I would if I'd lost my own dad."

It took a while, but finally he saw some softening in her features and then the gun come down.

"I still want an answer," she said.

"The truth is, I have no idea. I don't know your dad, I'm pretty sure. When did you lose him?"

"I didn't. He came down here last night. He left me in the car."

"You have a car?"

She hesitated. "Maybe. Whyn't you see my dad when he came down here?"

"Last night, you said?"

"That's what I said."

"You know, you have an unfriendly manner for someone asking a favor."

The gun came back up. "I ain't asking no favor, old man. Just you tell me!"

He sat back on his rump and grabbed his firestick and poked at the coals. "Sorry, that was rude of me. I could be more respectful, myself." He set a couple of small logs on to get the flames up. "I might know something about your dad, honey. But you've got to get rid of that thing."

He opened the large pack and pulled out a can of tuna and a can of spinach. He set the spinach aside. "No, that's probably a bad choice for a young girl." He took out a can of corn. "When was the last time you ate?"

He kept his eyes off her and went about the business of finding the can opener in the pile of contents that had been dumped from the small pack. He opened both cans, then dug out two forks. "You prefer hot or cold?"

"I ate last night."

"Nothing this morning?"

No answer. He dumped the corn into the pot and mixed in a little water from his jug and set the pot over the fire, on a cluster of small rocks that he used as his stove top.

"If you want any, the tuna will have to be cold," he said. "Heating tuna from a can doesn't sound agreeable to me."

"I'd as soon shoot you as eat," she said.

He chuckled, although he had to admit to himself that he didn't detect much bluff in the girl. She might just do it.

"I will tell you what I know about your dad. Just please give the gun talk a little rest and give me a chance."

When he looked up a moment later, the gun hung at her side.

"Well, I'm listening," she said.

He sighed, stirred the pot. "Ah..." He set the fork down on a rock and stood up slowly. "I'm sorry, honey." He thought he could see the reaction in her eyes before he said it. "Is your dad's name James?"

3

According to the girl, her father had told her to stay in the car, that he was going to walk ahead to check out the bridge. And he had told her that if he didn't come back in a quarter hour, she should take the gun he had left with her and go see the guy who was living under the bridge. Her dad hadn't come back, but she was not about to walk down to the bridge in the pitch dark looking for some old man. She had waited in the car all night.

She was a tough kid. No tears, no signs of profound grief at the news of her father's demise. Her lack of reaction told William that it came as no great surprise to her. He doubted she completely believed his story about the body floating away on the river, but she asked no further questions.

"I'm truly sorry," he said again.

She sat staring out at the river, knees locked in her arms, disinterested in his offerings of food.

"Do you have other family?" he asked after a time.

No response.

"Anyone who might come looking for you?"

She turned her face away to the downriver view and didn't turn back.

"Well, you can stay here, if you like. I would just say that if you need to go, let me know before you do. I know the area around here pretty good. I don't advise going alone, though. There are still some wandering yahoos in these woods, looking for good water or food or whatever else they can find, or steal. Any gas left in that car?"

"A little," she said, not turning to face him. "Not enough."

"Not enough for what? Someplace you need to be?"

Now she did turn to him. "You ask too many questions. You're nothing but a useless geezer. Maybe you killed my dad. How do I know you didn't?"

"I see. Well, I guess you'll have to take my word for it."

"I don't need nothing from you. You talk like a northern shithead. My dad would have punched your face in for breathing our air."

21

He finished the pot of corn and forked out the last piece of tuna from the can. He dropped his fork into the pot and set it on the ground in front of the girl. "Normally, I would tell you to take that down to the river and clean it. No work, no supper, in this camp. But considering your loss, I don't think that kind of thing is appropriate. You may do as you like. As for me, I'll settle for peace and quiet and maybe a nap later."

4

The nap came sooner rather than later, often the preference of men his age, he had learned. Not to his surprise, the girl was gone. At least she hadn't shot him in his sleep, although that wouldn't have been the worst that could happen.

The smoked turkey was gone, too, and one of his pocketknives—his favorite. His small pack had been ransacked again, albeit quietly and without much mess. Nothing else was missing as far as he could tell. Thankfully, not his revolver. Another trait of old age— carelessness.

She was on the move. She didn't have it so bad here, but perhaps she just didn't realize that. He had thought about taking it on the move himself, but he could never come up with an idea for a destination. Hopefully, the girl had one. One she could get to quickly before she ran into some bad shit.

To this point, his approach for avoiding the Big Question was simply to keep busy, mostly hauling supplies from the cache, fishing among the big bridge slabs with his little collapsible rod, cooking, reading the three paperback books he had, and just keeping an eye out up and down the river for signs of intruders. He had ventured into the woods a few times to scout for signs there as well, but also for scavenging opportunities. He hadn't had any sort of luck with the scavenging. But then the point was to keep

busy, to avoid the Big Question. Which was: Why did he bother to keep himself alive?

Chapter 3

1

HIS FIRST ORDER OF BUSINESS following his nap was to look for the girl's car. It was not hard to find, sitting on the shoulder of the road about a hundred yards from the bridge. Why she hadn't used the car to leave was a puzzle, unless she didn't know how to drive, or the car was indeed out of gas or close to it. James must have killed the engine and the lights and coasted down the hill to avoid being detected. How the girl's dad came to know that someone was living under the bridge was a question William never got around to asking the girl. It was something he should know.

The car doors were unlocked, and he practically took the vehicle apart looking for keys. But he found none.

He ripped out the back and passenger seat cushions but left the driver's in place, in case he might be able to use the car sometime. The cushions would make for a major improvement in his bed. The mirrors and some of the wiring might come in handy, but those, too, he left for future consideration. If he'd had the means, he would have gotten the car off the road and into a place of hiding.

Eventually, someone would find it and strip it down to a shell.

By the time he got back to camp, the sky had gone from blue to a high grey and the wind had picked up, tossing the tall oaks a bit and rippling the river water where it pooled under the bridge. He unpacked his tarp and set up a temporary frame for it out of a set of old aluminum tent poles, just in case things got breezy enough to whip the rain under the bridge. August storms in the Ozarks could get nasty. And as he watched the sky darken across the river and the clouds come rolling fast out of the west, he figured this could be one of those times.

Only moments before he heard the first thunder, he heard three gunshots from the same side of the river as the approaching storm. Flashes of lightening were now popping out, but no doubt that was gunfire, not thunder. He secured his pistol in his belt and smothered his fire with dirt. He gathered all his gear and food and threw the camo tarp over the pile. He hid himself in a stack of concrete, where a shallow overhang offered some protection from the rain and kept him out of sight from almost any angle. This was a first. The closest anyone had come thus far, except for the girl. At least, as far as he knew.

2

Despite his earlier nap, the steadily pounding rain, the crash of thunder, and the chill in the air, he was getting sleepy in his little hidey-hole. He would probably fall to sleep at his own hanging. It had developed into a habit, the last year or so, simply as a way of passing time—time that he was having difficulty filling. Retirement had that one drawback. It was a bad one, too. Boredom could be painful, even agonizing. The loss of TV and movies and the Internet made it even worse. On top of that, he should have brought more books with him to the bridge. One volume each of Marcus Aurelius, Emmanuel Kant, and Lao Tsu were not enough. His wife, before she died, had done her best to keep him occupied, scheduling activities that she seemed to pull out of the air and drop on him when he needed something the most. He lacked her touch for things social. Not that the Arkansas style of social was to his liking, but it could serve as a diversion now and then and a chance to increase his log of things to not like about the state.

The sounds of splashing from the river shocked him out of his indolent trance. Something frantic going on out there that he couldn't see from his little alcove. He decided to wait for it. He pulled his revolver from his belt.

Whatever was crossing the river was having a tough time of it. The struggle seemed to move from a little way upriver to a little way down, passing under the bridge, but also drawing closer to his side. When it stopped, he heard a faint, high-pitched groan. A human groan. Womanly. Then sloshing sounds as she climbed the bank, a few more groans, almost whimpers. She was above him, nearing his camp, when he poked his head out for a look.

3

"Looks like you might need something from me after all," he said.

The girl shivered beneath the blanket he had given her to cover herself after she had removed her wet clothes. Her lips were blue, her eyes not quite focused. Her smart-ass attitude was clearly overcome by a combination of physical distress and plain old fear.

"Two, you said?" he asked.

She nodded.

"Armed?"

Another nod.

"Who did the shooting?"

She tried to speak but gave up and gestured to herself, then to her pistol, which lay on the ground in front of her.

He picked up the gun and checked the cylinder, found three rounds fired and three more ready for whatever might come next. He set the gun back down, grabbed his sleeping bag, and draped that over the girl, as well. He coaxed her into sitting. "I won't lie to you. We have two choices: start the fire to make sure you warm up, or throw on layers in hopes that will be enough. If it's not, hypothermia could kill you."

"W-W-What's that?"

"That's when your body has gotten too cold to recover without help. I do believe the blanket and sleeping bag will be enough. I'll keep a close eye on you."

She nodded, seeming to understand that the fire option could prove foolish with a couple of gunmen in the area looking for her.

The rain was heavy enough to limit visibility to no more than a hundred yards or so. Unless her pursuers were well equipped for this kind of rain, he doubted they would maintain their hunt. They would look for cover, then maybe for the girl, or for signs of her, after the let-up. What could she have that they would want anyway?

He ought to put that question to the girl, but she was in no shape to answer.

He positioned himself back among the slabs, near his alcove, from which he had a good view upstream and down, where the rain was no immediate bother. Finally becoming aware that his blue jacket made him an easy target for eye or gun, he reversed it to expose the grey lining. Now and then he looked back at the girl, who was still shivering, but perhaps a little less violently. Shivering was good. When it stopped, he would have to do a closer examination to ensure things were heading in the right direction with her.

4

It was dark before the rain let up. The river had risen about two feet and could get higher. The current ran swiftly enough to deter any crossing, so they had that in their favor. And now the darkness, too. The girl would be fine. She even ate half a can of cold beans. He had laid out the car seat cushions to make a bed for her and borrowed back the blanket, which would have to do for him that night. No fire. Cold and damp air.

The girl lay on her bed, well covered by the sleeping bag.

"You know them?" he asked her as he sat on a rock near her bed. He kept his voice near a whisper.

She shook her head. "No, sir." Also whispering.

"Did you run into them by accident, then?"

"Yes. On the road."

"That's not good. The road is what everyone will prefer to use. Most likely they will hang around there for a while after dawn to see if you show up again."

That startled the girl and she sat up in her bed, her eyes darting upward toward the bridge gap.

"We would have heard from them by now if they had come this far on the road," he said. "They can't see us here from the overhang, anyway; the angle's not right. The river's too dangerous to cross now."

He took hold of her shoulders and lowered her back down onto her bed. "What did they want from you?"

She laid her head on her arm but said nothing.

"Silence tells me they did want something. Something you don't want to tell me about."

She glanced up at him. "You ask too many questions. I already told you that."

He chuckled. "Maybe I do. But it's good to know your enemy's motivation. That can help you figure out his next move."

She remained silent.

"Well, tell me this, then. Will they keep looking for you? Or is that the end of it?"

After a moment, she shook her head. "Don't know."

He chuckled again. "Oh, I think you know a lot you're not telling me. Guess I'll have to wait for it, though."

He rose to his feet and walked to his own bed. He tended to snore, so he thought it best to try to stay awake all night. Snoring might keep away the four-legged predators but would have the opposite effect on the two-legged kind. He sat on his mattress of sticks and grass with his back against the concrete footing of the bridge. Staying awake all night was not one of his talents. He mixed some instant coffee in cold water and forced himself to drink it.

5

Dawn came up a liquid muddle—roiling and tumbling water in the river, trees and the rims of the bridge dripping the last of the rain, the cold blue air thick and heavy. Normally he would stay in bed and wait for something better, but today was going to be different, he suspected. He stripped off his blanket and sat up, looked around for his cooking pot and pulled a bag of rice from his pack.

The girl had stayed put this time and was still sleeping. In the middle of the night, he had found himself in bed and under his blanket, not remembering how he had got there. He had thought to get up and resume his watch, but then asked himself why, that daily argument with himself returning: an angry instinct for survival shouting down the calm understanding that there was no *reason* to survive.

In a minor fit of frustration with himself, he ripped open the bag of rice, spilling some of it into the dirt beside the fire. His frustration mounting, he knotted the bag shut and stuffed it back into his pack. He set the pot aside. Breakfast today was going to be pre-made. A couple of chocolate Cliff Bars and two pouches of orange juice, straws included. He ate his and set the girl's next to her bed, then belted his pistol and quietly made his way down to the water's flooding edge. He rolled up his sleeves and then, submerging his bare hands and forearms, fished around the nooks and crannies of the rocks for a catfish. He had caught two flatheads previously, using that technique, but after a few minutes' effort this time, gave it up. He would have to cook anything he caught and, based on what the girl might tell him when she woke, a fire might still be out of the question.

He washed his face in the floodwater and rolled down his sleeves and climbed back up to camp. He sat near the girl and watched her easy breathing. She had a hardened look about her face, its origin possibly genetic in the way a lot of southern hill people appeared chiseled from the limestone of their hills. Or it might be the earned look of exposure to hard conditions or upbringing.

This girl was nothing like his own daughter. Carly was no princess, but she came into the world robust and tender and stayed that way. Living in NYC, married to a lawyer of means, she would continue in her fashion. Or, would have. The last he heard from her was a month ago. They had a plan, she said. A plan to get out, away. He didn't ask for details because he knew she wouldn't give them or would make something up to put his mind at ease. And he didn't want to know. He wanted to believe she had somehow made it out, perhaps in one of those private jets bound for the glories of the south seas.

6

"My dad was a drug dealer."

Her voice shook him out of another slumber, this time while sitting on his bed with his back against the footing. He looked over at her. She lay on her stomach, propped on her elbows but hiding her naked body with the sleeping bag.

"I thought it might be something like that," he said. "Those men, they were looking for your dad?"

"Everyone's been looking for him."

"He had something they want, then. Money or drugs?"

"Painkillers. A thousand bottles." She stared down at the ground in front of her for a few moments, then rolled onto her back. "He had it all hidden. He didn't know I knew about it, but I did. I even found where he hid it."

"So...those guys thought you could take them to it?"

She didn't answer.

"Painkillers. Makes a lot of sense. There's a lot of pain going around these days."

He stood up and handed the Cliff Bar and juice to her. "Breakfast."

Remaining well covered, she sat up and opened the bar and began eating.

"Your father knew I was here. How'd he know that?"

She shrugged. "I told him. My friend saw you. She told other people, too."

"Really? Common knowledge, then, around here?"

"Pretty much."

He started to his bed but turned back. "How many people are still hanging around here? How much food is out there?"

She swallowed hard and looked around for the water jug. He retrieved it for her and she drank.

"There ain't many. We run out of food when nobody had any more to trade us."

"Your dad traded the drugs for food?"

"'Course. Why not?"

He took the jug from her and capped it. "I don't want to ask you this, but it could be important. Why'd your dad kill himself?"

She looked up at him. "'Cause that's what people are doing now. Why not?"

"Why didn't you just tell those men what they wanted to know?"

"They woulda killed me after, that's why. Some of them eat people they kill."

"You've seen that?"

She hesitated. "I ain't seen it, but I heard about it."

Chapter 4

1

HE LEFT THE GIRL IN CAMP when he went back to the cache that morning. Mostly, he wanted to pick up some of the dried meat and more vegetables. The girl was undernourished. He found a little more than he bargained for when he got there. Scratching at the lids of one of the bins was a brown dog, about seventy pounds worth of what looked like a collie and lab mix.

The dog growled softly upon seeing him and backed a little further into the cave. William squatted and tried to coax the dog to him with hand signs and soothing vocalizations. Those settled the dog a bit but failed to draw him. He opened the lid of the nearest bin and pulled out a package of Slim-Jims. The act of opening the package was enough to peak the dog's interest. With a few enticing morsels tossed its way, the dog closed the gap and was soon eating from the hand. William petted it while it ate and checked out its sex. Female.

He sat down with the dog and spoke to it, petted it continuously, and eventually drew it close and hugged it. He was surprised it was so accepting. He had assumed that any animal left alive would be the one most wary of humans, probably gone half-mad from hunger and maltreatment. Food was paramount, however, overpowering even fear. Anyone who offered food you didn't chase off.

The dog followed him back to camp. Another pair of eyes, but especially a keen nose, was a fair trade in exchange for a little food.

The girl lay on her back under the sleeping bag and focused on a strip of smoked turkey, which she tore through with as much gusto as the dog did the Slim-Jims. William was not much of a meat eater himself, not red meat, but he had grabbed anything and everything he could carry from the store. When the girl rolled over and saw the dog, she jerked backward and pulled the sleeping bag tightly around her. Her eyes signaled a level of fear William had not seen yet in the girl.

"Don't blame you," William said to her as he set down his pack. "But this dog is a lot more easy-going than anyone else you've met lately."

"What? He don't bite?"

The dog walked immediately, though cautiously, over to her bed and sniffed it out. William, meanwhile, pulled a can of peas and a plastic spoon from the pack.

"No, *she* don't bite," he said. "Give her a little piece of that turkey and she'll be your best friend."

He sat down on the rock near her bed while she hesitantly followed his advice, pulling her feeding hand quickly away from the dog's mouth. "If people knew I was here," he asked the girl, "why is it no one came for what I have?" He finished opening the can of peas and held it out to her. "Don't forget your vegetables."

She sat up, careful to cover herself, took the can and spooned out the peas. "You're just an old man, I guess," she said, after a couple of mouthfuls.

"Old men aren't entirely useless. Some of them must have known who I was, where my house was. They were probably customers at my store."

The dog sniffed briefly at the peas but showing no interest sat down next to William.

"Are you the storekeeper, from out on 371?" the girl asked. "I been in that store."

"Yeah? I don't remember you."

She went on to finish the peas and handed him the empty can. "You got any kinda dessert?"

He laughed. "You think this is a restaurant? Let me check with the cook. Maybe there's some apple pie left."

"I wish." She turned her attention to the dog. She pointed. "He yours?"

"He is now, I guess. Well, like I said, he's a she."

"That's okay." She gathered the sleeping bag and sat back against the bridge footing, hiccupping a couple of times. "Most of the dogs has been eaten around here."

He nodded, stroked the dog along her back, randomly searching for ticks.

"I didn't, though," the girl said. "I could never eat a dog, but I did eat robins and mice. My dad was a good hunter."

"I suppose."

After a moment she said, "I didn't like eating them things. They didn't taste too bad, but they was...like...innocent, or something."

"Yeah."

2

When the sun broke out, he spread the girl's clothes across the rocks to finish drying. He grubbed around in a nearby patch of weeds and plucked out a pair of grasshoppers, always plentiful in August, then took up his fishing pole. He hooked and dropped the bait about four feet below the water's surface, where he guessed the catfish would be feeding close to the bottom. The floodwater would bring out the big ones. He had no sinker, only a pebble crudely tied to the end of the line. He had to rely on feel for the bottom. In low water, he usually settled for small sunfish.

The dog followed him down to the river and lapped her fill and sat beside him. In better times, he would have enjoyed this scene immensely. It almost brought tears to his eyes to think about it. His own little girl had gone fishing with him a few times. They even had a dog, Riley.

That was Minnesota. Lake fishing. Walleyes. From a canoe, usually, but also from the dock at Pelican Lake. God, he was seventy-two now. When that much time passes, the memories pile up so deep it becomes hard to find your way back to any particular place and time. The details get lost. They get replaced by emotions. The places and times get all confounded and distilled into feelings of regret or sorrow. Why not joy? Why do the good feelings slip away?

Nothing biting. Slow action leads to too much thinking when you have a fishing pole in your hand. *What the hell was he going to do with this kid?* Suddenly, he had become a caretaker. He was too old for that now. He had forgotten how it was done. It didn't seem appropriate, somehow.

"Hey, old man," she called down to him. "You mind if I—"

"William is my name," he answered.

"Oh. Do you mind if I have some more turkey?"

"No. Not at all. Thanks for asking first."

"Huh? Okay."

3

Back in camp, fishless, he found the girl dressed. Her clothes were still a bit damp, but in the afternoon heat, that was no problem. She stood propped against the footing, arms folded, staring out at the river.

"Will you take me?" she said.

He collapsed his fishing rod and set it down.

"Take you? Take you where?"

"To my aunt's. My dad said you would take me."

"Uh, first I've heard of that. Who's your aunt?"

"She lives in Reeds Spring. Her name is Linda."

"Reeds Spring. Isn't that up in Missouri somewhere?"

"I think so."

He grabbed his food bag and pulled out the last smoked turkey package. "Man, you went through a lot of this."

She looked at him like he'd said something rotten. "So? You said I could."

"Yeah, well, I'm not saying you did something wrong. Now, what's this about your aunt?" He opened the package and started in on the dried stick of turkey.

"She lives in Reeds Spring."

"I got that part, but why would we want to travel all the way up there? It's going to be the same there as here. Could be worse."

"My dad said she has a...I forget what it's called. Maybe it's a...a compact, or something. A place people can be safe."

"A compound?"

"Yeah. I think that's what he said."

William sat down on his bed and stared at the remains of his lunch in his hand. "Well, lots of people had ideas like that. Some, I'm sure, even built them. But compounds are not all they're cracked up to be. Few of them ever were successful, or would be successful, in the current situation."

"Why not?"

"Lots of reasons. People living there don't get along. They're expensive to build and maintain. The idea of being able to hold off the world, even with a lot of weapons, doesn't compute."

"Dad called it a secret place."

"Yeah, maybe they thought it was, but that's another thing: secrets don't stay secrets for long. A compound is a fool's idea of paradise."

She walked over to him. "Maybe not. Besides, I don't want to stay here forever. How much food you got anyway?"

He couldn't argue with the girl's basic logic. "Enough for a while."

"Then we should go right away, before it's all gone."

He didn't know how to talk to this kid, any kid, about those realities. "We're…better off here. Better than trying to walk all the way up to Missouri with killers running around."

"They're gonna come here, too!" she shouted. She walked away and plopped down on her cushions. He let her be for a time, while he did the math again on the food supply. Another mouth to feed, now, and a dog. Kids and dogs ate more than they needed to. It was their nature.

He probably had to cut in half the remaining time they had. That would be a few months. They would run out about the time winter came in. The worst time for that.

"What your name, by the way?" he asked her.

"Who cares?"

"Well, I could call you by your real name, or just make one up. I think I'll call the dog Riley."

She was slow to get back to him. The dog offered no objection. It lay down beside him.

"Kathryn. They all me Kat...old man."

4

"You tore up our car," the girl said, a little angrily and fingering the seat cushions. A long period of silence between them had preceded that.

"Yes, I did."

"Why?"

"Looking for the keys."

"I have the keys." She pulled them out of her jeans pocket and rattled them. "Anyway, there ain't hardly any gas left."

"So you said. Why are you upset about it, then? It made a nice bed for you."

She slapped one of the cushions she sat on. "You call this nice!"

"Kat, don't bite the hand that feeds you."

It appeared to take her some time to grasp his meaning.

"I really want to see my aunt. My dad said they have tons of food, and even gas for cars."

He stroked the dog. He was glad for her company, like having someone on his side in a fight.

"That car is likely to draw some attention at some point," he said. "I may need your help in disguising it."

"I don't even know what you are talking about. I asked about going to my aunt's. Who cares about a car with no gas in it?"

"People with guns, looking for you."

"Then let's go!" She let out a moan of exasperation and laid down on her bed. "Go. Before they get here."

He spent the rest of the daylight gathering wood from the vicinity of the car and stuffing it into the interior. He set up a start-point inside with a small bird nest surrounded by kindling. He would set it ablaze in the wee hours, when no one would be around to spot either smoke or fire. At least, that was the theory. When he got back to camp it was almost dark and the girl was gone, his stuff untouched, as far as he could tell. He wandered along the riverbank up and down, flashlight in hand but not wanting to shine it. It was the girl who spotted him.

"I'm tired," she said, repentantly. "Can you help me get back to the bridge?"

He found her sitting in a pile of large river rocks. With the aid of a revealing beam from his flashlight, he sat down with her. "Look, Reeds Spring could be anywhere in Missouri, maybe two hundred miles from here. I've never been there. I don't know how to get there from here. Your car had no roadmap. We would need to get directions somehow, then make our way through miles and miles of woods and hills and across rivers. There's a bunch of big lakes up that way, too. Bridges might be down, even if we wanted to use a road to get across the tough spots. When…if…we got there, most likely it's going to be bad news. Most likely the compound, if that's what it is, will have been overrun by all kinds of bad actors. Hell, even good people would try to get inside. Think about what your aunt and her friends would do to keep them out. For their own survival. It would be a mess."

"How do you know that?"

"Well, you're right. I'm only being logical. There is some chance, I suppose, that the place would hold together. It's a slim chance, though."

"I ain't stupid…sir. I know our chances here are nothing."

5

"How much can you carry?" he asked her.

"I don't know. Probably as much as you."

He laughed. "Well, the packs aren't big enough to weight either of us down. I've loaded in the light stuff, left out the cans." He handed the girl the smaller pack.

He ran ropes through the blankets and sleeping bag so they could be carried over their shoulders. Lighters, flashlights and batteries, some of his spare clothes, knives, guns, all the essentials would be going along. "It hurts to leave the rest behind," he said, "but we don't exactly have a truck. Not even a horse."

"I know."

"Sure you do. But I bet you won't miss this place."

She didn't answer.

"Look," he said. "We might encounter some dead bodies along the way. That's probably more than likely."

"I seen some already, by the roads."

"Yeah. Just keep your eyes out for a spare set of shoes, or boots, that will fit you. Those sneakers on your feet aren't the best for hiking and won't hold up for long."

"I'm glad Riley is coming. She might find something, the way dogs do. But isn't Riley a boy's name?"

"That doesn't bother me if it doesn't bother you."

She shook her head.

6

North was the general direction. His $75 compass gave him that with first-rate reliability. But there was an immediate need for a road map or other map of the border area. A general direction wasn't good enough. They needed a precise direction, and they needed detail. They would stick to the least developed areas, the national or state forests, once they could identify where they were.

The river had retreated considerably from the day before, so they crossed it right there at the bridge. From there he led her and the dog through the dewy morning woods near enough to the road so they might spot an abandoned vehicle or other potential source of booty. The going wasn't easy with all the underbrush to fight through. Kat asked repeatedly if they might use the road. "What happened the last time you tried that?" he finally said.

He had heard that some people could estimate miles covered on foot with surprising accuracy, just by dead reckoning. He doubted he had that talent. Even so, he tried to keep a running count, mile by mile. When his count reached six, well into the afternoon, Kat made her first complaint about her feet.

"If it wasn't so important to keep you healthy and cooperative," he said, "I would remind you that this was your idea. So no complaining."

"But what am I supposed to do if they hurt?"

"Yeah, well, sometimes you're right, I guess. It's best if you let me know when something hurts. We both need to hold our shit together or neither of us makes it. Excuse my language."

"Hah. I've heard it all before. I could say "fuck" around my dad. He didn't care."

"Really? Well, don't try that with me again."

They stopped for a rest in an open, grassy area where a small stream crossed their path. They drank. The road lay quiet about two hundred yards to their left. He had been checking it frequently but there was no sign of a vehicle or abandoned house that might hold a map.

"My dad said you can get sick from drinking outdoor water," Kat said.

"You can. It's unlikely in these streams, though. This time of year, in the Ozarks, those with surface water are spring-fed. Drink all you can."

He had brought along the half-gallon jug but kept it mostly empty to lessen the load. He carried it tied to his backpack.

While they sat in shade beside the stream, William took hold of one of Kat's feet and felt around the edges of the shoe. Then he pulled some little blue stem grass from several patches growing nearby. With his hunting knife, he cut the grass into six-inch strands. "Take off your shoes," he said.

He stuffed the shoes with the grass. "Take out what you need to keep them from being too tight."

She fussed with them for quite a while, standing and sitting, walking around.

"Okay now?" he asked.

She nodded. He stood up and they started off again, Riley leading the way toward a distant hillside of tall white oaks and cedar groves.

7

The first night out passed in reasonable comfort. He decided against a fire, which they didn't need for warmth. A massive pile of oak leaves served well enough for a mattress, his blanket and her bag enough to keep out the night air. They had ended the first day exhausted. She fell asleep half a minute after finishing a packet of smoked salmon and two handfuls of crackers. He wasn't far behind. A tired body had a way of soothing the mind. He imagined neurotropic chemicals being released by his muscles and flooding his brain. Fine with him. It was possible this dying on the move idea was indeed a better one than sitting around waiting for it. The thought was somehow satisfying.

Morning found him stiff and sore and more than willing to complain if he could find a nurse or doctor around. He had a small stash of pills in his bag for emergencies but was not willing to employ them for anything less than the worst kind of discomfort. For her part, Kat seemed fine except for aching feet.

"You going to be able to walk?" he asked.

"Sure."

"Here." He tossed her a Cliff Bar.

She caught it. "Great." Which pretty much summed up his own feelings about Cliff Bars at that point.

He thought half a day of hiking through those woods would be enough for day two. That would give them more time for rest until their bodies adjusted. They could quit around two o'clock. Long before that, though, Kat claimed to see something on the road. He pulled her down with him as he knelt behind some honeysuckle.

"Where? I don't see anything."

She pointed. "There. It's shiny."

He changed his angle of vision and picked up the sunflash off...something. Something perhaps three feet wide. Not exactly in the road, however. It lay on their side of the road, maybe ten yards from the strip of blacktop.

"Let's wait here a bit," he whispered.

Five minutes passed with no sign of movement from or near the object. He pulled out his pistol. "Listen, we should have talked about this sooner, but if anything happens to me on this trip...." He hadn't thought that through for himself yet. "Well, you either go back to the bridge or you keep going north. Try to find someone else who can help you."

She grabbed his shirt sleeve. "Don't let anything happen to you."

"Sure. That's what I'll do. You stay here while I have a look."

He removed her hand from his arm and set it on Riley's neck. "Hold his collar," he told Kat. "Her," she replied. He nodded and raised up and moved quietly and slowly toward the target, eyes dancing in all directions around it. The woods were stone quiet but for a distant thrush and the crunch of his feet on oak leaves and twigs. Nothing moved but him, which could be either a good thing or a bad thing.

The flash proved to come from a road sign that had been knocked off its wood post and tossed over the gutter. Something violent had snapped the post in two. Further along the ditch, he saw tire ruts leading toward the trees, a few small trees down, and then the wreckage—a sedan with its front end bent upward and raised three feet off the ground against a large oak. Looked like all the windows were busted out; both front doors hung open. What appeared to be two bodies lay on the ground outside the driver's door. They were stripped of their clothing, most of it anyway.

He stepped up to the bodies and nudged them with his foot and found them stiff. A man and a woman. Young, perhaps in their thirties.

Bugs of some kind crawled out from under the woman, whose torso lay beneath that of the man. The movement raised a stink. He turned away and looked inside the car. Either it had been ransacked or this couple kept one helluva messy car. Paper and plastic bags and wrappers all over the place. Nothing under the seats. Nothing in the glove compartment or behind the visors. A pile of paper in the back seat included a national forest map. Mark Twain National Forest, it read at the top in fancy letters. Not a topographic map, just one of those superficial, eye-catching tourist maps with a lot of green on it. But it was something. And it was all he could find of any potential value. He got himself out of there without further delay and hurried to rejoin the girl.

8

Distracted by a flood of questions from Kat, it took William a while to make sense of the map. He knew the Mark Twain National Forest had various sections scattered around southern Missouri, so that name did nothing to place them, and the names of towns and highways located on the map were unfamiliar to him. But finally he located the name of the lake winding snake-like through the forest area: Table Rock Lake. That would be the one north of Eureka Springs. He'd talked to fishermen who boated and fished up there. The name Kimberling City at the edge of the lake rang a distant bell. What the map did not indicate was the name Reeds Spring.

No matter. If they wanted to travel unnoticed in Missouri, best to do it through a national forest. In the girl's mind, based on her father's talk, Reeds Spring was not some place far away, which meant most likely somewhere in southwest Missouri. Anyway, they might yet come upon a decent road map, a map of the whole state that would tell them exactly what they needed to know.

So, keep heading north. They would cut Highway 62 up there eventually, and Highway 62 ran east-west from Harrison to Eureka Springs. So, follow 62 to Eureka Springs, then turn back north to the forest. Cross the state line along the way. It was the only reasonable plan possible at the moment.

9

The practice of keeping a road in view as they traveled the woods seemed a good one. No chance of getting turned around that way, and it offered the possibilities of salvage from the road. Of course, a road might bring them trouble as well if they weren't careful. Roads meant houses, towns, and other things that would be better to avoid unless they were desperate.

William called it a day when Kat began tenderfooting her way along. "Okay, it's all right to complain," he told her. "Let's settle here until morning." By his system of reckoning, they had covered another four miles that day.

The spot he chose offered plenty of cover and no shortage of dead oak leaves for bedding, which they gathered into two piles. "Did that dead lady have good shoes?" Kat asked as she unrolled her sleeping bag.

"No, Kat. They took everything from those two. Everything."

"You think they were killed in the crash, or after?"

He shrugged. "I didn't care to look into it.

"How much of that sort of thing have you seen?" he asked after a moment.

The girl lay down on her bed. "My dad shot two people who was sneaking around our trailer."

He sat himself on his own bed and called the dog to him. He began fashioning a leash from a strand of rope he pulled from his pack.

"I seen my school burned," Kat said while he worked on the leash. "We was driving by it and people was carrying stuff out of it. There weren't kids in it though. Mostly, my dad was keeping me in the house."

"That was good."

"When they started burning the houses, my dad quit the stuff he was doing to get food. That's when the men came around that he shot."

"Painkillers for food, you said?"

"Yeah. It was real easy at first and he didn't get no trouble, but then things got bad and he got robbed and people didn't have much food to trade us."

"He told you about me, then, huh?"

"Not until we drove out there to your bridge. But it didn't matter 'cause I already heard about you. One guy talked about going out to get you. I think he meant kill you and take your stuff."

"Didn't know I was so popular. I've kept to myself pretty much since moving here." He looped the leash around Riley's neck. "Good dog," he said.

They were quiet for a time, then he noticed the girl was sleep-breathing. He hadn't put together a late lunch for them yet, but he decided to let her be. He took a tube of anti-bacterial lotion from his first-aid kit and rubbed it on a nasty scrape he had picked up along the way. One infection, even from a minor wound, could muck things up for them. He had a few band aids and bandages in the kit, his supply of ibuprofen, antibiotic pills, and cold and fever meds. But the supply line was broken. Broken for good. Nothing was going to last long, as they had all believed it would only a few months ago.

Chapter 5

1

MID-MORNING THE NEXT DAY they came upon three houses clustered around a rural intersection of what appeared to be two county roads. They sat and observed for the better part of an hour before William decided to initiate his own crime spree. Expecting to have to break and enter, he found the back door of the first house, a single story with red brick façade, torn from its hinges.

Anything in the house's living and dining rooms that wasn't demolished had been carried off. He did find a fork and two spoons lying near the door, probably dropped by whoever last left the place. The TV and every other electronic device was stripped or gutted or simply crushed in place, signs of more than basic thievery—the vandals wanted to take out their anger on something. One day they would no doubt turn on each other.

The remains of an elderly woman lay on a bedroom floor amid the shreds of a mattress. Not much left to her but hair, bones, and a dress. Animals had taken the rest.

The Buick in the garage had also been tossed, its gas tank lid left dangling, the tank unquestionably siphoned dry. But, *holy shit*—a road map of Arkansas lay on the floor with other debris from the glove box.

Back in the house, he quickly checked the kitchen cabinets and cupboards and found them empty. The mess of useless rubbish in the basement convinced him not to waste any more time on the place. He did take the power cord from the TV.

The second and third houses provided a leaky canteen, a can of bug spray, a shoe lace, and three old hardback novels by Robert Louis Stevenson. He chose *Treasure Island* and left the other two. And, like his predecessors, before leaving, he ditched the canteen.

2

The insect repellant proved a godsend for William and Kat that night. The spot he had picked out for camp must have suited the mosquitoes as well, for they swarmed and buzzed relentlessly. But few struck. The marauders at that last house must have had an aversion to DEET. He was not so afflicted. He lay on his back staring at the starlight through the patchy growth and cloud cover, then followed the moon for a while when it broke through. A peace of mind supplanted the usual fervent worry that accompanied most waking moments when he wasn't active. He tried not to think about all the things that could kill him in the morning, or the day after. Or how he might react if something happened to the girl, or the dog. His wife had instructed him in mindfulness.

As a youth he had practiced yoga long before it became the panacea of the western yuppie, and in middle age rather intense meditation. And it was all good. But he had fallen out of the habit. His recent efforts to revive the discipline had mostly failed, although the 30-minute mindfulness technique introduced by his wife took him some of the way back.

Marian had been good for him in many ways. He knew that while she was alive, and he'd often told her so. But her reaction to compliment or sentiment was never very sharp. Deep down, she felt it—gratitude and love and those kinds of things, he was sure—but verbal expression was a different matter for her. She cooked for him, shopped for him, did his laundry, and freely offered help when he was jammed up by some mundane technical problem, like a misbehaving computer. She was a giver, not a taker. A doer, not a talker. In all, she had been the best match a man like him could hope for.

Her death had ripped a hole in him. Four years ago, now. He had suddenly found himself with only two people in the world he would call friends, and he saw them a couple of times a month, at best. He had wanted to sell the house, but it was a house she loved, and it held part of her in it. He tried traveling a few times, twice to Europe and once to the Yucatan, but other than visiting historic sites he found little to do in foreign places that was different than home. The people seemed just as bland. They were good people, compared to what he generally ran into in Arkansas, but they went about their daily business oblivious to an American from the Midwest with mysterious motives and a defeated look on his face.

Sleep finally caught up with him and he woke with first light. He let Kat alone and busied himself with fashioning a sleeker leash for Riley from the TV cord. He felt the wind come up—from the southwest, according to his compass. The hazy sky foretold of rain. He hadn't thought much about bad weather. Shelter could be as important as food. Somehow, he had to anticipate what trouble might come from the sky.

He laid the roadmap out on his blanket, located his home, and traced with his finger the route he believed they had taken north. That road they had been following was likely Hwy 103, which would lead them up to Hwy 412, and that, as he had guessed, would take them to Hwy 62. He quickly searched the northern border of the map along the thin strip of Missouri, hoping to find the name Reeds Spring, but came up empty. The national forest there was clearly marked, however, north of Eureka Springs.

Following roads had its advantages, but they seldom ran in straight lines and he and his company were constantly adjusting course to keep 103 in sight. Early on, the highway bordered woods, but lately it had opened into a more pastoral landscape, forcing them to take chances with quick traverses of grassy fields or deviate further from the road and stick to the woods. Lots of time and energy was wasted trying to keep the road in sight. He would think about changing strategy. They might do well to short-cut some of the turns by cutting overland.

3

"William," the girl said, finally awake. That was the first time she had used his name. "I think my feet are better today."

He finished rolling up his blanket and studied the sky through the tree cover. Still gray. He felt at the bottom of his pack for the tarp, to reassure himself he hadn't forgotten it.

"Glad to hear it," he said, "I'd like to do another eight hours of walking today, but you tell me if things are going bad for you. Anything from your feet to your head, if you know what I mean."

"My head? What could be wrong with my head?"

"Oh, boy. Well, maybe nothing at your age. You wait."

She shouldered her pack and sleeping bag and they set off. Riley appeared glad to be moving again, as he seemed capable of going all day long. The dog preferred to run ahead, typically between ten and thirty yards, rarely out of sight.

"That Riley is a good dog," Kat said.

"Sure is. Maybe he'll get us a rabbit one of these days."

"I ate lots of rabbits. My dad hunted them down on Farmer Wayne's place. He said the rabbits liked the farmer's spinach garden, which was why he let him hunt there."

William chuckled. "No spinach gardens in these woods."

After a couple of hours, William noticed that the road was now following a creek and that the prevailing slope of the land had turned from uphill to down. Another godsend.

By noon they had crossed two dried streambeds pointed toward the creek. Their water jug was down to a third full. The slow-moving air seemed filled with the wet stuff, however, and sooner or later it was going to come out.

When a somewhat aged and decrepit farmstead appeared, William's first thought was to look for a pump, which he then spotted just outside the back of the barn, near the cow pen. Again, they watched a considerable time before moving in. And again, he went in alone. He checked the cow's water tank and found it full, so water was flowing. At the pump, he expected a squeak when he raised the handle, and a squeak he got. A loud one. As the water flowed into the jug, he kept his eyes on the house about fifty yards away. Jug full, he eased the handle down, then slid into the barn through the back door. A lot of heavy old equipment lay around, but he saw nothing useful to them. He hurried to the big doorway in front and glanced at the house again but saw nothing moving there. He passed on the house and retreated to the woods.

"They's cattle bones over there," Kat said, pointing as soon as he arrived.

The white bones were scattered around a small clearing that intruded into the woods. Some still carried bits of dried flesh. A large pile of ash from a fire sat in the middle of the clearing.

"We've got no use for those," William said. He led her and the dog deeper into the woods.

4

He called a halt to the hike at 4 p.m., where a spring-fed stream cut their path. It ran a mere trickle but enough to allow them to preserve their jug water.

They had passed several more farmsteads and crossed a dozen small pastures and barbed wire fences. Any garden or field with crops, even immature crops, would have been stripped by now, so he hadn't bothered to look for those.

Rest followed a small meal. Riley wandered off somewhere. William felt a big nap coming on, but then the bark. Riley.

"Damn it," he mumbled, climbing to his feet. He stepped past Kat and eyed the woods. "We don't need that," he whispered.

He pulled his gun and turned to Kat and gave her the stay-put sign and then, bent low but moving quickly, he scooted through the oaks and undergrowth while straining to identify what might be out there.

Another bark. Then a series of barks.

Then human voices. Male. And not that far away.

A moment later, Riley came running out of a patch of cedar, directly toward him. He corralled the dog, pulled the new leash from his pocket and slipped it on the animal. He looked behind to see if Kat was in view but didn't see her. He hunkered down where he was.

With his arm around the dog's neck, William could feel the low rumble of a growl starting up. "Lie down," he whispered into the dog's ear as he pulled her to the ground. He lay flat there with the dog tight at his side. "Quiet, girl," he whispered.

A moment later he saw the figures of two men intermittently through the brush, coming his way. When they cleared the cedars, he had a good look at them. They wore filthy overalls and baseball caps. Both were bearded. One carried a shotgun, the other a small pack.

They came to a sudden stop. Looking well to William's right, one of them said, "Well. Check this out."

William followed the man's line of sight and saw Kat walking out of the trees. Riley squirmed as if she wanted to go to Kat, but he held her down.

"I believe we have us a girl, here," one of the men said.

"Kid," the other said. "But a girl kid."

Kat had nothing with her. No pistol. Unless that was a pistol in the back of her jeans.

She stopped about ten feet from the two men.

"Got us a girl," the one said to the other. "Where's your dad?" he asked Kat.

"Ain't got one," she answered.

"Mom?"

"No."

"No dad, no mom. The fuck you doing out here?"

"Walking my dog. Did you hurt her?"

"We seen your dog, but he run off. Don't you run off now."

"Why should I?"

"Well," the other man said. "If you don't know that, then I guess we'll have us a party."

The two men stared at Kat quietly for a moment as Kat stared quietly back at them. Then the one with the shotgun started toward her.

Kat reached behind her and drew the object from her jeans. She pointed the pistol at the man and fired off two quick shots. The man dropped to the ground with his gun like a sack of rocks. She then aimed at the other and fired once. He groaned, stumbled backward, then he too went down. She hurried over to them, picked up the shotgun, checked the load, and snapped it back shut.

William took a few seconds to catch his breath.

"Hold your fire, Kat," he said finally as he stood up. He made his way over to her, eyeing the downed men. He checked each of them for a sign of life. The second man had a faint pulse but had stopped breathing; the first was clearly dead.

He turned to the girl. "Jesus, Kat."

Chapter 6

1

THEY LEFT THE BODIES and the heavy, double-barrel shotgun where they had fallen out in the woods and waited for night, saying nothing to each other for a long period of time. William petted the dog, then pulled together another cold supper of dried meat, crackers, and a salad made from plantain and dandelion he had found in the pastures. The girl didn't touch the wilted salad. He found a couple of suitable trees with forked trunks and cut and jammed a sapling between them to serve as a support for the tarp if they should need it during the night.

"I've lived on this planet a long time," he finally said to her as dusk fell and after he had retreated to his bed, close to hers where she sat staring into the woods, as if waiting for something other than sleep. "I've seen a lot of things that were hard to believe, but a kid your age doing what you did I can find no way to accommodate."

She looked at him. "I don't know what that means."

"It means I don't understand why you killed those men, the way you did."

"Huh? They was going to rape me."

"Are you sure of that? Were you sure of that when you shot them?"

"I probably saved your life."

She looked away and went quiet for a few moments, then turned back. "Yeah, I'm sure they was. My dad taught me. We practiced. He said if I thought a man was gonna rape me, that I had a right to shoot him, and I better do it quick, 'cause a man is always bigger and stronger."

"Your dad had you practice shooting people?"

"'Course. Me and Emily, my friend. We had a hay bale back of the trailer for practicing on."

"But this is the first time you actually did it, right?"

She nodded. "'Course. I don't go around shooting people."

He shook his head. "Well, you practiced well, I'll say that."

They were quiet again until the dark took over, each sitting on their separate bed of leaves. William sprayed his hands with the repellant and wiped it over his face and forearms, rolled his sleeves down, and slid under his blanket. He tossed the can of repellant over to Kat.

"You mad at me or something?" she said.

"Ah...no, not mad. Just...astonished, I guess. Bewildered."

"'Cause I shot them?"

"I suppose. Although I might have done the same if I was in your shoes. I understand how you've been taught, and that the times are...desperate, and desperate things must be done. It can be a shock to witness is all."

"I don't understand *you* sometimes. The old men I've heard talk never sounded like you. They mostly smoked or chewed and told stupid stories, about the old days or whatever."

Kat lay down and pulled her bag over her shoulders. Riley unwound from his tight curl in his spot between them and went to lie down beside her.

"How were you in school?" he asked.

"I was okay. I quit after fourth grade to do home schooling."

"Home school. Your dad?"

"Yeah. Mom was already gone. But Dad was good at it."

"How's your math?"

"Good enough."

"Six times four?"

She hesitated. "You think I'm stupid, don't you? It's twenty-four."

"Stupid, definitely not. Being smart and having a good education, though, are different things. What happened with your mom?"

"She left. She and dad fought. I guess she didn't like it."

"Where'd she go?"

"Memphis, I think. That's in Tennessee. Ain't too far away, but she never come back."

"No letters or emails to you?"

"No. I never missed her, anyway."

2

Next morning, they were on their feet and moving early. According to William's dead reckoning, they had covered a total of about 18 miles, as the snake crawls, since the beginning of their journey. According to his map, as the crow flies, it was more like 10 or 12, assuming they were getting close to Hwy 412. At Hwy 412, he had a decision to make at a branching of the road.

For now, they had rain to deal with. The morning carried in a slow drizzle, huge drops but well-spaced, which they were able to ignore until close to noon, when the skies darkened with real purpose. As he had done the night before, he rigged a tent-like frame between a pair of forked trees. He laid the tarp over the frame, securing it with stones they carried from a nearby stream. They heaped their usual leafy beds beneath the tarp, this time one large bed. It would be close quarters.

"You okay with this?" he asked Kat.

"With what?"

"Us sharing a tent and a bed."

She shrugged. "You don't scare me."

"Oh. I don't?" He laughed. "I'm not sure what to make of that."

She shrugged again. "You snore some."

"Yes, I do. Stick an elbow in my ribs if you have to."

3

The serious rain didn't start for an hour. From there, it built steadily for another two, then went on until dark. They had napped that afternoon, the dog snuggled under the tarp by their feet, and by night William was wide awake, as was the girl.

"I have a plan for us," he told her. "Pretty soon we are going to leave the highway and follow a stream that will cut quite a few miles off the trip. We'll take a forest road that follows the stream. We'll have a good supply of water nearby and there shouldn't be people to worry about that far from any towns or highways. You good with that?"

She didn't answer for a few moments as she lay on her back and stared up at the tarp, perhaps listening to the "slap, slap" of the rain against it. In the darkness, he could make out her outline, as close as she was, but not her expression. He sat at the opening of the shelter behind her.

"Sure," she said.

"That will get us close to Highway 62. Then Eureka Springs isn't much farther."

"I been there. That's a funny town. We had pizza there and I bought a used book."

"What's funny about it?"

"It's like squeezed down into a canyon or something. You can walk through it in five minutes, but it's got like a million stores. My dad and I had our picture taken wearing old-time clothes. There was lots of people walking around for a little town."

"Tourist town, then?"

"Yeah. We was tourists. But we didn't have much money. Some people carried bags and bags of stuff they had bought."

"What book did you buy?"

"I think it was a kid's book. I was only about nine. I never read it."

"Your dad didn't read it to you?"

"He read me books when I was little, about five or six, when Mom was still there. He quit when she left, and he started doing illegal stuff, with selling drugs."

"You knew about that then?"

She shifted position beneath her bag, onto her side. "No, but I figured it out later. Cops came around a few times. He got mad at them. He said they was asking for too much money."

"Ah. So, money was hard to come by for you two?"

"I guess. We always had food, though. He was a good hunter."

"Back at one of those houses I picked up a book you might like. It's *Treasure Island*, by Robert Louis Stevenson. It has pirates and treasure and adventures on the high seas. I could read that to you, when we stop for camps along the way."

She appeared to think that over. "Maybe."

4

Late morning of the next day, after they had hiked through more miles of pasture and woods, over the creek several times on tiny bridges, and passed a number of burned-out houses and farms, William sighted what looked like the 412 junction up ahead. A bridge lay between, with a sign reading "Osage Creek." Beyond that, open fields spread far and wide on either side of the road. Directly beyond the junction was a steep hillside, the new road running east and west along its base.

He told Kat to stay behind while he scouted. He would wave his shirt as a signal for her to come ahead. The fields had been planted with red clover and were flowering robustly. It was nice to see at least one form of life doing well. At the junction, the road signs read "412" left and right, "103" left. Sitting beneath one of those signs, with his head hanging between his knees, was a man wearing a dirty straw cowboy hat, faded jeans, and a green jacket. The jeans and jacket were both dirty as well. After a quick debate with himself, William pulled his gun and approached the man. Not until he got within fifteen feet did the man hear the clump of his boots on the asphalt. His head and arms jerked free of his knees and he scrambled to his feet.

He was a big man, six-five perhaps and heavy. Young—early twenties it appeared. His eyes were white and wide as clam shells. Despite the man's large proportions, his clothes seemed over-sized.

William didn't say anything right away, just waited to see what the man's reaction might be, which was basically nothing. No sudden movement—no movement of any kind but breathing and blinking his eyes.

"I have a gun here," William finally said, "but I don't intend to use it."

The man swallowed hard. "I-I...." He raised his hands to his side, waist-high.

William waited, then said, "I'm passing through. I've got no problems with you if you have none with me."

The man shook his head.

"You waiting for somebody?"

He shook his head again. "I...I'm just here." His voice was high-pitched for a man his size.

"Just here? Not waiting for anyone?"

"No."

"Do you have a weapon?"

"No, sir." He started to open his jacket.

"Slowly."

"Yeah." He complied, revealing nothing under the jacket but a blue denim shirt, stained with sweat.

"Okay. I'll take your word for it. You traveling too?"

He shook his head.

"What are you doing here, then?"

"Well...." A long pause followed. "I guess I'm just tired of it. I think I would like you to shoot me."

William stared at the man. "What?"

Tears filled the man's eyes. "I would appreciate it."

"Jesus."

William continued to look him over. The young man had that sad sack look about his face and posture that made a good match to his doleful plea. "When was the last time you ate?" William asked.

"Uh, maybe a week ago. I-I thought someone might come by here and he would...do it for me."

"Kill you?"

The man nodded. His face contorted into a grimace and he lowered his head, put his hands on his knees, and began sobbing.

William put his gun back in his belt. "Yeah." He looked back down 103, where he saw nothing of Kat or the dog, then to his left, down 103/412. The next road sign there was hard to read, but it appeared to say, "Rudd 8 mi." That agreed with his map.

"How long you been here," William asked.

The man straightened up. "Couple days."

"No one's come along?"

"Not till you."

William pointed down the west-bound branch of the road. "You been down that way?"

The man looked. "I came that way, yeah. My bike ran out of gas."

"You cross a bridge, over a stream, a mile or so down?"

He nodded. "Yes, sir."

William took a moment, breathed and sighed. "Come with me, then. I've got some food. You got a bag or anything?"

The man pointed into the clover. "I tossed my stuff in there."

"Dig it out, then, and follow me."

5

His name was Mathew, though he preferred to be called Matt. Kat and Matt, William's growing family the beginning of a Dr. Seuss title. In one sitting, Matt put a sizeable dent in their food supply while they sat in a tree break at the edge of the clover field.

"Are you from around here?" William asked, when Matt had finished his Snickers bar.

"No, sir."

William waited for more, finally asked again, "Where from, then?"

"Branson. I lived in Branson."

"That's the country music tourist town?"

"Yes, sir."

"What'd you do there?"

"Country-rock."

"You played music, you mean?"

"I tried out for the Texas Tenors, but they didn't take me."

"I see. You were a singer."

"They said I was too young. But maybe I wasn't good enough."

"I heard of them Texas Tenors," Kat put in.

"Your hometown?" William asked Matt.

"What, sir?"

"You say you lived in Branson. Born and raised there?"

"Joplin. I was born there."

"You have any idea where Reeds Spring is?"

"Reeds Spring? Yes, sir. It's not far from Branson. I sang there a couple of times."

"East or west of Branson?"

Matt stared at William, as if he was trying to work out the directions in his head. He seemed not quite "with it," perhaps befuddled by lack of food or from stress.

"North, sir, I think. But not far. Maybe fifteen miles, I think."

"Branson is on the big highway, right? Hwy 65?"

He nodded. "But I wouldn't go there if I was you."

"Well, we were planning on going to Reeds Spring through Eureka Springs, but now that sounds like a mistake." William pulled out his roadmap, although already knowing that Hwy 65 was to the east of their current location. He spread open the map so that Matt could see.

Matt turned away from the map, as if he had no interest. "Highway 65 is full of trouble" he said. "There's gangs over there. They have bikes and gas and a lot of guns."

"Do you have a suggestion?"

Matt turned to the map.

"I would take this way," Matt said, tracing with his finger.

"By road?" William asked.

"I don't think I would go by road. But maybe, if you want."

"It's not easy through the woods," said William. "Up and down hills, through brush. There aren't clear trails for us, at least none that I know of."

"I know some trails, up in Missouri. This road here," Matt pointed to the blacktop in front of them, "this 103, will take you to Blue Eye. I know some forest trails up there. The trails ought to get you to Reeds Spring."

6

So, they would stick to the basic plan, only cut the trip shorter by continuing on 103 north of the 62 crossing and forgetting about Eureka Springs.

William agreed to take Matt along. Possibly, the guy wasn't yet thinking straight, or perhaps he was just bullshitting about knowing the trails and just wanted to share their food, but it seemed a risk worth taking.

In the meantime, Kat's shoes were the main problem. They were coming apart at the seams, especially where the tops met the soles. Matt went through his gear and pulled out an old shirt and tore off several strips. With his pocket knife he cut away the canvas tops of Kat's shoes, then poked holes in the edges of the soles and ran the strips of cloth through those, fashioning a pair of sandals.

"Cool," said Kat. She tried them on, tying them down several times to get the right feel, and walking around. "I can live with it," she said.

"Tell the man thanks," William said to her.

"Sure. Thank you, Mr. Matt."

"Be sure and keep your socks on," William added. "The grass and brush can do a number on your feet that way."

West on 103 they almost immediately came upon the gravel road that the map showed running alongside Osage Creek. This was the shortcut William had promised Kat. Damn, maps were great. It told him this road would get them back to 103 in five or six miles, cutting an equal number off the original route. They walked the road for a couple of those miles, then came upon a concrete bridge over the creek. They set up camp in a small turnout there which had probably been used by fishermen.

7

Matt had his own sleeping bag and was out cold within minutes of lying down, before the sun had set. Kat followed soon after. Neither had asked for supper, although William thought Kat had probably raided the candy bars while he was searching for a camping spot. William emptied his gun of its bullets before laying it next to him and drew his blanket in close. The young man seemed okay, but who knew.

Come first light all seemed in order. Matt and Kat still slept. He did a quick inventory of their food and some even quicker mental calculations, concluding that it was unlikely they had enough food to last them all the way to Reeds Spring. The day dawned orange and clear except for a few low clouds in the east that filtered the sunlight. He reloaded his revolver and rolled up his blanket, which was now getting filthy from heavy use. He checked his pack for the plastic soap container and found it. He wandered over to the stream to have a look at the water, then back into camp.

For breakfast, it was oat bars with some powdered milk mixed in cold water in his cooking pot. They passed the pot around. "We'll have to ration the food," he told them. "You can do all of us a favor if you don't ask for extra, and if you don't exercise your creativity by slyly sneaking extra. Leave the food decisions to me."

"You think I been sneaking food?" Kat asked sharply.

"Only you know about that," he answered. "I'm talking about from here on. We need each other and we need peace among us. It's still a long trek ahead."

"How long?" she asked.

"Fifty or sixty miles," I estimate. "If we make six or seven miles a day off-road, a week or more. If we use these backroads and park trails, we might cut that down by a couple of days."

"Sounds good to me," Matt said. "Sir, thank you for letting me come along. I'll try not to eat much. God bless you."

William nodded to the young man. "For now, before we start out, you two need to do something else for me."

"What's that?" said Kat.

He waved to them. "Follow me."

He led them to the spot on the stream he had visited a little earlier. He pointed to the pool that gathered around and under the sprawling roots of a huge sycamore.

"You might not recognize it, but that's a bathtub. You'll need to wash your clothes as well as your bodies."

He handed the soap container to Kat. "You go first. You walk into the water fully dressed. You take your clothes off piece by piece and scrub each one with soap, rinse it well, then toss it onto those roots there. Then you wash yourself. When done, you put those wet clothes back on and come back to camp. I'll have a fire going. Dry you off in no time."

They looked at him like he was crazy. Kat pointed to the water. "That's gonna be freezing."

"Be quick but thorough. Gotta be done. Me, too, when you guys are finished. You'll be glad for it."

Chapter 7

1

THE FIRE PROVED LESS EFFECTIVE at drying out their clothes than William had hoped, but at least it warmed the occupants who, by the time they reached the camp, were shivering to their bones. As soon as practical, they smothered the fire, collected their things, and returned to the road. The road had been quiet all night and morning, but sometimes trouble came on quiet feet.

Not far along they encountered what was left of a burned-out pickup. Matt said it looked like a ranger's pickup; William had no idea. The tires had been taken and the headlamps and tail lights as well. When they resumed the hike, William noticed Riley sniffing the weeds at the side of the road. He took a quick look, saw the decomposing body and the ranger's badge, called the dog to him, and kept moving.

The road crossed the stream several times with low-water bridges. Passersby had taken advantage and tossed all kinds of junk into the water at those points. Why it was that, given the choice, idiots preferred to toss their refuse into water rather than just onto the side of the road, or for that matter into a garbage bag, was a mystery William supposed would never be solved.

He was thrilled at the progress they were making by open road. Walking was still walking but dragging through heavy woods seemed like insanity at this point. Especially the uphill stretches.

Kat's sandals were holding up to the gravel. Matt seemed well suited for this kind of thing, even though weakened by days of hunger. A youthful body was an amazing thing, and William often became painfully aware of how long ago that had been for him. His health was good, maybe even excellent, but he felt things these young ones did not.

"Where're you from?" Matt asked William as they walked.

"Oh, well. I'm a transplanted Minnesotan. Been down here about eight years now, but I still don't know the state all that well."

"Me neither."

"So how did you end up here?"

"My brother. He and some of his buddies raised a pole barn. They fixed it out with concrete walls and gun holes and freezers and a generator. And they had gas tanks and all kinds of other stuff. They started on it two years ago. Henry, my brother, said bad times were coming."

"Survivalists?"

"Yeah, I guess that's what they're called."

"And you came to join them?"

"Yeah."

William hesitated. "You don't have to talk about it, if you don't want. But what happened?"

Matt was slow to answer. "Uh, nothing much worked the way they planned it. The freezer conked out. The gas tank ran dry 'cause someone was stealing it. People outside was trying to get in and they lit fires and it got too hot inside to stay there. There was lots of shooting when we came out. I made it into the woods."

"Did you shoot somebody?" Kat asked.

Matt shook his head. "Well, I shot at somebody, this guy. But I'm pretty sure I missed. I ran outta there. I guess I was a chicken."

"They let you go?" Kat asked.

"I threw down my rifle. I thought they would come and get me, but I guess they weren't that interested."

"I shot a couple," said Kat. "Just the other day."

"Nothing to be proud of, Kat," said William.

"I know that. I ain't bragging about it."

"You two know each other pretty well, then?" said Matt.

"Not very long," Kat answered. "I found William living under a bridge. Just a few days ago."

"Oh, I thought he was your grandpa, maybe."

"Hell no. I never met my grandpa, either one. They was dead, I think, when I was born. Or maybe off in prison. Lots of kids I know have relatives in prison. 'Specially since drugs got popular."

William laughed. "Drugs have been popular for longer than I have been alive."

"Painkillers?" said Kat.

"Not so much. Heroin. Cocaine. Even LSD has been around for decades."

"I heard of that," said Kat. "Makes you go crazy. Take your clothes all off and jump out of windows."

"Well, the stories about some drugs are crazier than the drugs, or the people who use them."

"Not you, though?" Matt asked.

William wasn't sure if he should answer truthfully. "Okay, a few trips on magic mushrooms these last few years. Only marijuana before that, when I was younger."

"Mushrooms?" said Kat.

2

What sounded like a long roll of distant thunder could not have been. The sky was clear in all directions.

"Hear that?" William asked the others as they walked.

"Bikes, I think," Matt said.

William led them into the woods, the dog on her leash, away from the stream and far enough to give them a good lead if they were somehow spotted. They waited in a small gully with limestone outcroppings on either side. But bikes or no bikes, the thunder-like sound did not return.

"Could be someone saw the smoke from our fire this morning and came to check it out," William said. "My guess is they rode the blacktop out on 103 for a quick look around, then moved on. That fire was dead out, wouldn't you say, Matt?"

"I think so."

"The bad news is that they are in the area. We're a long way from Highway 65. Let's sit and wait it out."

The woods along this road were thick with downed trees and cedar groves and underbrush and ruggedly cut with small gullies like the one they were hiding in. William sure didn't want to have to give up the road.

"What will they do to us if they find us?" the girl asked.

William shook his head. "Who can say. Rob us, for sure."

"Kill us?"

He shrugged.

"They would," said Matt. "They might eat us."

"Don't scare the girl, Matt. Some of what you hear is nonsense."

"I ain't scared of that," said Kat. "What's the difference, if you're dead?"

"The lesson here is just to be extra careful," William said. "The fire was a bit careless of me, even though we needed it."

"I have an idea," Matt said. He smiled. "Let's not take any more baths."

They all laughed. "A solution to every problem," said William.

They waited another thirty minutes before William led them back to the road. From the edge of the woods they checked the road both ways and waited another few minutes before resuming the trek.

"Only thing that worries me," William said, "is that we didn't hear the bikes drive back the way they came. Could be they stopped somewhere out there on 103."

"We'll hear them good if they come this way," said Matt.

"Yep. Big advantage there."

But there was no thunder, no bikes, and within two hours they reached the junction of the gravel road and 103, where 103 completed its loop to the west and came back to a northerly course.

3

William was spoiled now. Road-walking was just superior, that was all there was to it.

"Let's get some sleep," William said to the others as they lay stretched on their bellies beneath the low-hanging bows of a sprawling cedar. The cedar stood in an otherwise open area and thirty yards off the highway. Riley lay beside Kat, her grip on the leash firm, her willingness to take on the job of dog manager most welcome. The shade was also welcome on a sunny afternoon, and the cover was ideal, as the heavy bows reached nearly to the ground. "We'll walk after dark, take the highway this time," William said.

"You said that was dangerous," said Kat.

"Yeah, I said that, didn't I? I also said we shouldn't do anything careless. Talk me out of it, then."

She gave him a strange look. "You're supposed to be the boss."

He winked and smiled at her. "Only as long as you allow it. You just challenged my decision. What's your idea?"

"Stay off the road. They have motorcycles."

"Anyone riding a motorcycle at night will have his headlight on. We'll see it a mile away, probably hear it before that."

"Up on Highway 65, they sometimes had lookouts," Matt put in.

"Is that something you saw, or something you heard?"

Matt wavered. "Just heard."

"Would you sit out here on this nowhere blacktop waiting for some desperate tramps to come along in the middle of the night? How would you get the news to others even if they did?"

Matt started to speak but gave it up with a shrug.

"What if we come to a town?" Kat asked.

"We go around it." William's back was beginning to ache, so he rolled over and looked up into the thick growth of cedar. "Couple more things. Those sandals of yours, Kat, aren't good for much more forest hiking. A town might provide boots. You can go barefoot on the blacktop. Can your feet handle that?"

"Sure. I go without shoes all the time. I have tough feet."

"We'll keep out of the sun, traveling at night," William went on. "We've been lucky to have a lot of overcast lately."

"I don't really understand where we are going," said Matt.

"Reeds Spring," said Kat.

"I know that. But what's there?"

"My aunt Linda."

Matt gave Kat a long look. "Okay. Has she got food?"

William laughed. "Kat's aunt is holed up in a sheltered compound up there. At least that's what Kat tells me. Hope she's right."

"You think I lied about that?"

William laughed again. "Kat, you have what some call a hair trigger, a temper button. I'm figuring out how to set it off."

"I know what a hair trigger is."

"Try to sleep, guys. It'll be a long night on the road."

4

A few hours later, closing on six o'clock, William's backache woke him. He employed a few of the stretching techniques his wife had taught him but that he had later given up. Not much effect, as before. He crawled out of their little den and walked around a bit, bending in all directions, cursing a little for the timing of this kind of intrusion. He knew the scenario. Nothing he could do would make much difference. His body would take two or three days to solve its problem its own way, the improvement coming on gradually. Walking would be painful but doable, if his load wasn't too heavy. Any sort of lifting was out of the question. Movement would have to be slow and easy. Not what he wanted right now.

On his way back to the cedar, he noticed a smoky haze to the north, drifting through a valley between two wooded hills and across the highway, across their direction of travel. Water vapor haze wasn't likely, this time of day. He studied the haze for a sign of direction but didn't see any movement in it. At the cedar, he eased himself beneath the boughs and slid under, finding Matt awake and Kat still asleep.

"You hurt?" Matt asked.

"Back trouble. I may need your help."

"What should I do?"

"Can you manage a heavier load when we hit the road?"

"Sure. What I got ain't much. I can take your pack."

"That would be excellent."

He couldn't find a comfortable way to lie on the uneven ground, although he tried every posture he could imagine. "Matt, I'm going to slip into those woods over there," he pointed across the highway, "and make my way up to that notch there between the hills. There's something I want to check out. I need you and Kat to stay put, and to be quiet."

"Something going on?"

"Nothing to worry about. I just want to be sure about something. I'll be back in an hour."

He climbed out of cover, then turned back to Matt. "Listen. If I don't come back—I mean now or any other time—I need you to watch over the kid. Get her to her aunt, if you can."

Matt nodded.

"I heard that," Kat said, her back to them.

William and Matt looked at each other. William smiled.

"You know that's what they always say in the movies," William said to Kat. "Just following the script here."

"Whatever."

5

The first uphill grade William encountered made it clear that his plan was hopeless. The back simply wouldn't have it. Wincing and cursing, he staggered back to the road and across to the hideout.

"Nothing doing," he told them as he slid under the cedar boughs. Kat and Matt were lying on their bellies and had been watching his approach. "Can't do the hills right now."

"Why do you want to?" asked Matt.

William pointed north to the haze. "That doesn't look natural to me. Could be fire. Probably is fire."

After eyeing the spot for a moment, Matt said, "So, you wanted to make sure?"

"Basically. We don't want to wander into somebody's camp accidentally."

"I bet they aren't friendly," said Matt.

"Could be an empty camp," said William. "Tonight, we'll see the firelight if it isn't."

William dug through his pack and pulled out a couple of the ibuprofen pills and washed them down. "Shit," he said. Then, "Sorry, Kat."

"God. My dad said that a hundred times a day. And worse."

He nodded. He searched for the best way to lie and thought his right side worked best. He wrangled some spare clothes under the side-bow of his back for support.

"I can do it," said Matt.

That caught William by surprise. "You mean, check out that smoke?"

"Yes, sir. I know my way around the woods. I'm big but I know how to be sneaky and quiet."

"I could do it, too," said Kat.

"You stay with me, Kat," William said. Then to Matt, "Most likely it's nothing to be concerned about. We can just wait it out."

"I'd like to, though," said Matt. "I ain't scared the way I was before. I was ready to die when you found me. I should be dead now. What I got to be scared of now?"

William gave it some thought. Of course, that was true for all of them. They had nothing to lose but a few more days or weeks or months of life. Years were in serious doubt. Matt gave the impression of someone not especially competent in delicate or complex situations, but he probably did have some backwoods savvy.

"All right," William said. "But keep in mind that your safety comes first. Don't take any chances. See what you can and get back here with no fooling around."

"I got that." Matt scrambled from cover.

"And no hurrying!" William urged.

6

Night came in like it had better things to do, slow and grumbly. But no Matt. The glow of the fire up ahead brightened as the sky darkened, painting the hills temporarily in orange hues. William thought he heard what might have been muffled screams but convinced himself those were imaginary. Sure, there were people up there, probably just having a good time.

William preferred not to talk about the situation with Kat. But Kat was relentless with questions.

"I'm sure he's fine," William told her several times. "A lot of things could delay him. He might have waited too long to start back and got caught by the dark."

"Think he's lost?"

"Probably, a little. He's smart, though. He knows what to do when lost in the woods. The smartest thing is to wait for light, so you don't wander too far off course."

"I don't think he's very smart," she said.

William gave her the look of a father set to recite the law of the house. "Kat, I don't know how long I will know you after this, but it won't be long if you don't learn something about common manners and selflessness."

"Huh?"

She turned away from him and lay on her side, putting her arm over the dog.

"We have no choice now but to wait," he said. "If he isn't back by—" He stopped himself. *Shit.*

"By when?"

William sat up. "Change of plan," he said. "Get your stuff together." He began collecting his own and felt the twinge in his back, although the ibuprofen seemed to help. He left Matt's things where they lay.

"What now?" the girl asked, seeming reluctant to get up.

"We're moving. Not far. Just to another hiding spot."

"Why?"

"Kat, cut the questions for now. In fact, I want silence from now until daylight. It's important."

"Right," she said, with little enthusiasm.

With help from the moon's light out of the low eastern sky, he led her and Riley across the road and into an area of tall timothy grass that edged the woods. From there they would have a good view of the cedar hideout about a hundred yards away and would be virtually invisible to anyone on the road.

"What about Matt?" Kat whispered.

"We'll see him if he comes. The moon will be up till dawn. Keep your stuff together, in case we have to move quickly. And you have to keep the dog quiet if we see anything."

"How do I do that?"

"Put your hand over his mouth and pull him close to you, gently."

"Her, not him."

William nodded. "Yeah. Whisper to her to be still. It's worked before."

They settled in. William scrounged around inside his pack and located a Snickers and handed it to Kat. "Sleep, if you can," he said softly.

"You said to be quiet. And I'm not sleepy."

"Good, then. Eat something and shut up."

7

William spent half the night pacing the edge of the woods behind their lookout. The pain of lying down was too much to put up with for long. At times, he had to rely on Kat to watch the road, a task she seemed to take seriously.

He hated the lack of information and his inability to control the situation. The bridge had been easy. Just him. Not going anywhere. He knew the area like he knew the age-spots on his arms—not pretty, but not cancerous. He should have enjoyed the absence of purpose there. It could have been liberating, allowing him to simply take what life gave him in the moment and not fret about the future.

Thinking, however, always led him to places he didn't want to go. Fretting about the future seemed hardwired into him, right alongside regretting the past. He had become more and more embittered, a miserable ass no one would want to be around. He should admit to himself that it was worse under that bridge. Hell, it was worse back at the house. The trek kept him occupied through purpose. Purpose was a good thing. Wasn't it?

"There's nothing out there," Kat said quietly, but with some exasperation, when he rejoined her. "Nothing gets really boring."

"You'll think boring is paradise if we do see something."

"What's wrong with you?"

He put his fingers to his lips. "If we're not going to be quiet, we need to stick to whispers."

"'Kay," she whispered.

"It's my back. It's hurts."

"Why?"

He snickered. "You'll have to ask my back."

"You are weird. If you *were* my grandpa, I would probably disown you."

"Well, grandkids don't *own* their grandparents, to start with. It's the grandparents who do the disowning, which means cutting the grandkids out of their wills."

"Whatever. We probably wouldn't get along."

"Hmm, maybe not. Maybe I'm not so bad when you get to know me. I gave you a Snickers."

She giggled. "Oh, thanks a lot."

8

When the first light of dawn began to emerge, William heard the shuffling and scraping sounds of many feet moving through the woods to their left. He grabbed Kat by the shoulder to hold her down and put a hand over his mouth as a signal.

"People coming," he whispered. "Do not move."

He then pulled Riley in close and wrapped the dog's mouth in one hand while pulling his pistol with the other. He wasn't sure how good their cover was from that direction, but it was all they had.

Four men advanced in a slow-moving arc through the oak trees to the forest's edge, about forty yards from their lookout. The men were obviously trying to be quiet about their business. They stopped there. Each appeared to carry a gun. At least one of the guns was an automatic. Riley squirmed, but pressure on her mouth and a squeeze to her ribs settled her.

The men wore camo clothing, from hats to boots. One of the men pointed to the big cedar across the road, then gave the hand sign to advance. He led them out of the woods with a voiceless charge that ended abruptly in the ditch at the side of the highway.

Each man then raised his weapon and opened fire. Rounds tore into the little cranny where he and Kat and Matt had taken shelter. The firing went on and on. They were intent on destroying whatever the cedar might be concealing. Riley burrowed her nose into William's chest, no doubt frightened by all the noise. Finally, the leader called it to a halt. All four walked across the road, guns pointed in front. One of them fired a couple more rounds into the tree boughs. The leader turned to him and waved him off with the words, "Enough, shithead." They cautiously lifted the boughs to open the concealed area to view.

"Fuck!" one of them yelled. "You kidding?" said another. A third pulled out some of Matt's gear and examined it, then tossed it back under the cedar.

They jabbered and gestured at one another but beyond William's hearing, perhaps arguing a little. One threw up his hands. Another said loudly, "Let's cut that fucker down and kill him again."

After a moment, they shouldered their arms and began walking up the highway to the north.

"They're leaving," William whispered to Kat, stating the obvious. She nodded her head.

They watched them disappear around a bend of the road.

Chapter 8

1

THEY LAY UP IN THE WOODS for two days while William's back worked out its issues and while the route ahead of them cleared of trouble, if it was going to clear.

The smoke up that way had not been visible since that first night. William and Kat had in fact heard bikes rev and fade away to the north the morning of the shootout. At noon this day, William went to investigate on his own. What he found wasn't anything he wanted Kat to see. Matt had been strung from a tree branch by his arms, brutally disemboweled and partially skinned, his swollen mouth stuffed with grass and mud, his feet cut off. William immediately turned away and walked back to Kat, using the road and fighting back a tear or two. This was what the world had become. No law, no justice, no punishment for the most heinous mistreatment of fellow human beings. Members of the same species destroying one another for short-term gain, or just for the fun of it. Why had he become so embittered? Pretty damn obvious. He half wanted to shoot himself right then and there.

Kat and Riley were where William had left them, and despite the urge to get going again and leave the shit behind them as soon as possible, staying put a little longer seemed sensible. Riley brought back a grey squirrel after a romp into the woods. William would have loved to cook it for Kat but was unwilling to start a fire. Riley got the whole thing. When asked by Kat what had happened to Matt, William said that he found no sign of him and thought it most likely Matt simply wanted to take his chances on his own, or that he had some other place he wanted to go. Kat asked no further questions.

They hit the road at ten o'clock that night. Kat put away her sandals and seemed to enjoy the foot-freedom that afforded. The chances of meeting up with the biker gang again was a haunting thought, but at this point William was unwilling to give up the road for the woods. After a few miles, the woods on both sides of the road thinned out and the landscape became increasingly dominated by crop fields and pastures. Or so it appeared under a bright moon. When a road sign read "Green Forest 1 mi," he finally diverted course and took a farm road running parallel to the highway. A back entrance to the town, perhaps.

2

The angular grey outlines of buildings up ahead announced the arrival of the town. It was near three in the morning. He left Kat and Riley on the dark side of a small shack at the edge of town and made his way building to building for a quick scout. The absolute absence of human beings was an amazing thing. The absence of lights, any kind of noise, even if only the hum of electrical transformers, gave the world an unearthly feel, even though it was how the world was made to be. As he passed another storefront, he tripped on something—a small can of peaches, if he was reading the label correctly in the moonlight. Unopened. "Really?" he said quietly to himself. He kept the can and peered into the store but could see little except what looked like shelves. He opened the door and let himself in, taking out his flashlight.

Some of the shelves held contents, although most were empty boxes and crates sitting in various states of disorder. He found a second can of peaches, however. Who would leave peaches behind? He walked through an interior doorway and discovered more boxes strewn about, some shelves tipped over, and all kinds of clothing lying on the floor. It was women's clothing. Blouses and skirts, socks and shoes.

Shoes!

Damn, all types of shoes. Nothing suited to the tastes of the bikers, he supposed. Along with the peach cans, he threw a couple pairs of jeans, socks, a sweater, and three tops into an empty box. He scavenged for boots and found several pairs. He threw them all in.

One more examination of the shelves revealed nothing else that he wanted to carry. If nothing fit the girl, then he could come back. He picked up his box of loot, clicked off his light, and left.

2

She tried everything on, some of which fit well enough and some of which didn't. He couldn't see well in the moonshadow of the shack where they quietly went about the business of wardrobe tryouts, but Kat seemed to know from the feel. One pair of boots did the job for her, providing she wore a second pair of socks with them. That was good enough. This wasn't the Mall of America. They dumped whatever she couldn't use or carry, including her old clothes and makeshift sandals.

They headed for what looked like a tree-covered hillside about a quarter mile east of town. They burrowed into some brush, made some space for themselves and settled in to wait for morning and the next day.

"I feel good about these clothes," Kat said. "I never got new clothes much. We always went to the place with used clothes or Goodwill."

"I'm happy for you," he said.

"I guess I'll miss the sandals. I guess I'll miss Matt, I mean."

"Yeah. I'm sure he's okay."

She looked at William with what might have been a stern expression on her face.

"I think he was a good man," Kat said after a few moments.

"Seemed to be. He didn't give us any trouble. He was helpful."

"He liked Riley."

"I believe he did."

Another hesitation before she spoke. "Just don't say he's okay, anymore."

3

The town of Green Forest was quiet all day, even though it was located at the junction of Highway 103 and the bigger Highway 62. Between their hideout and the town's first buildings lay numerous skeletons—cows, but perhaps horses as well. Ash circles nearby suggested they had been eaten on the spot. Just outside the town was a demolished poultry farm, one of many they had seen on their journey. It was hard to imagine the chaos that took place in one of those barns when the starving vandals broke in.

The landscape in that area was largely open, with pastures extending up into the hills. Those houses and trailers not in the town proper were all burned out. Why not burn the entire town, while you were at it? Why burn at all, when you've already stripped the place of everything once necessary or dear to the inhabitants? A kind of Viking funeral for the entire concept of hearth and home?

Neither of them slept especially well that day, just off and on. Time dragged. The sun shone brightly and the heat took its toll on William. His back felt much better, but his endurance now began to come into question. The sweat seemed to drain the energy from him. He hadn't done anything like this in many years. His body wanted rest, even when it rejected sleep. He had lost count of the days and the miles, although he now had the map to give him good estimates. Ten long miles to the next town. Oak Grove.

They held up on supper until they were ready to go. Ten o'clock again. Another cold supper. A mockingbird above them ran through its catalog of songs and seemed like it would never quit. One more reason to hit the road.

And it was another productive night, although Kat's feet eventually developed a few hot spots and they stopped to apply Vaseline. They stopped again near dawn when the town of Oak Grove finally came into view. They made another camp well off the road and away from buildings. They waited for yet another nightfall.

Chapter 9

1

THAT NIGHT it was Kat who spotted the oddly shaped signs up ahead and beside the road. On close inspection, one read "Welcome to Missouri;" the other, "Mark Twain National Forest."

"Well done," William told Kat. "Now find the one that says: "Reeds Spring."

"Oh, sure. You find that one."

"Okay, I'll settle for "Trailhead."

They waited out the remainder of the night and rested, nesting in their usual way on piles of leaves and under tall oaks and with the tarp handy in case of rain. It felt good in some way to be in Missouri, even though he knew it was no less dangerous than Arkansas. Evil knew no borders.

At first light and after a little scouting, they found the first trail about a quarter mile farther down the road. Arkansas Highway 103 was now Missouri Highway 13. William found it pleasant to be traveling in daylight, beneath tall trees again, and surrounded by the odors of nature. But only a short distance into the forest they came upon a body. William told Kat to keep going while he examined it for anything useful. "I can help," she said. "No, keep going."

The man must have died of something natural, as there were no signs of violence that William could see. His backpack held a sleeping bag, some aspirin, a Swiss army knife, a cheap compass, a lighter, empty water bottles, and a few other items of no use. He'd exhausted his food, no doubt. Most important, the map pocket contained a trail map. William kept only the aspirin, the lighter, and the map. He stripped the shoelaces from the man's boots and used those to replace his own, which were wearing out.

Kat was waiting for him a hundred yards ahead. He opened the map and showed her with his finger. "We take this trail north. It follows Highway 13 pretty closely, see. We will come to this town called Lampe, then we branch off a little to keep a northward course. Here we will come to a bridge that spans this big lake. We probably have to use the highway to cross on the bridge."

"What's on the other side?"

"Look here. Highway 13 takes us through Kimberling City, then up to the end of the forest. There at the border is the pointer, see? It says: "to Reeds Spring.""

"Holy cow. Are we close, then?"

"A lot closer. Wish it had a mile marker on it."

"Will it be safe?"

"That's the plan. We'll stay on the trails. We'll let Riley do his thing and run on ahead a bit. He'll warn us of anyone coming the other way."

"Good. I like that."

"When we leave the forest, we'll have to go back to night-traveling the roads, or maybe through the woods along the roads."

"Okay. Along the roads in the woods is harder."

"Daytime on the trail, nighttime on the roads, then."

She nodded. "Matt said he knew the way."

"Yeah. We got our trail but lost our guide. This forest map will work, though."

2

The trail proved flatter than William had expected, following stream courses, which lowered the grades. Backwoods homes and small chicken farms became common sights not far off the trail, most bordering small pastures. None looked habitable, most utterly ravaged. He saw few indications of recent human activity on the trail, although the rains of late could have obscured footprints or mountain bike tracks. A food wrapper here, a few cold and ashy campfire sites there and there, was all they came across. More birds in these woods, though. Riley, running out ahead, probably spooked any ground-dwelling critters.

"This is like a Sunday hike with the family," he said to Kat.

"Nah. My family didn't hike. What's the fun in it?"

"Fun? Hmm, I guess I mean it's a break from the stress of daily work."

"I ain't never had daily work."

"Hah, me either, lately."

"'Sides, I been feeling more scared since them bikers."

"Sure you have. That's perfectly normal, Kat."

"I didn't sleep much last night."

"Bad thoughts in your head?"

"Yeah. Plenty."

"Well, your dad would be proud of you. You've been a picture of courage."

She was quiet for a time.

"Mostly, I'm worried that Aunt Linda won't be there. That her com...compound will be ruined. Maybe she's even dead."

"Whatever we find, we will deal with it."

3

By late morning the land had opened into numerous pastures with tree breaks running through. The breaks offered their best option for concealment during their transit of the open areas. Obviously, this "forest" was well occupied by private lands in a kind of mixed-use arrangement.

William estimated they were about four miles into the forest—a slow pace due to the need for frequent breaks to treat Kat's foot abrasions—when they came upon a branch in the trail, and a sign indicating the town of Lampe was 2.2 miles ahead on the right branch. They stopped to eat.

"What, exactly, is a compound?" Kat asked.

"It can be a lot of things. There are different kinds. Most are built in such a way as to hide them, to keep them secret, somewhere in the woods. They usually have room for quite a few people. Some are built in caves, others are underground with only a door or two showing. Those are called earth shelters. They are usually stocked with a lot of food and have water nearby. And a toilet somewhere."

"What if someone tells a friend about the compound, who tells someone else, and so on? How do they keep it secret?"

"That can be a problem, for sure. Also, everyone has to get along pretty well."

"My Aunt Linda isn't so easy to get along with. She slapped me once when she came to visit, when I was six."

"Some relatives are stricter than others."

"Did you slap yours?"

"No. I made no hitting a rule for myself."

Kat slipped her boots back on. "Good you didn't."

They loaded on their packs and bedding. Kat whistled for Riley, who crashed and tumbled out of the brush. She held a chipmunk in her teeth and insisted on flaunting it proudly in front of them. She ran up the trail with it.

"That dog eats better than we do," William said.

4

As they neared Lampe, the main trail began to follow watercourses around steeper and heavily wooded slopes. It bypassed the town, which was fine as they were well supplied, no further shopping necessary. William popped open the cans of peaches at supper in a small clearing called Douglas Glade on his map. They rested, then decided to stay the night, the grass there being lush and soft. A starry sky and rising moon imparted a feeling of hope in William that he hadn't expected or experienced in some time. Another miniature gift from the gods, perhaps. He wished they would send him a big one. He reflected on the wonders of a universe so vast and mysterious as that revealed in a night sky or in numerous books he had read on the subject. He had studied cosmology and physics in college and maintained an interest all his life. He knew that the true workings of that great sphere were yet to be fully understood by science. With each new discovery came a realization that the mystery ran yet deeper, that there was ever more to be learned. Recent findings hinted at a universe that was mere illusion, a projection of no substance, designed by a grand intelligence existing somewhere beyond the bounds. He was never religious. He found all the world's so-called "great religions" to be equally absurd and childish, as well as dangerous breeders of destruction, but a scientific path to a Higher Intelligence had become available, and he was not opposed to checking it out. Unfortunately, at present, the players in this great game of the universe were making a mess of it.

Kat and Riley lay not far from him, quietly sleeping pictures of innocence in the world. That's how all people came in. Living is what broke some. Disappointments, pain, and suffering. Perhaps some of the faults were programmed in the genes, a sort of built-in guarantee that life wasn't meant to be without trials and conflicts; but living in the chaos had its own effects. Kat was no angel. She had been distorted to a degree from the ideal already, at age fourteen. But the deeper blamelessness showed through still. She had a right to a full life, if she wanted it. Was it his purpose now to help her achieve that?

5

Morning dropped a heavy dew onto the clearing. Songbirds chimed in. Regular alarm clocks, they were. The sky paled to a mix of blue and crimson. William lingered in his blanket, at one point coaxing the dog to join him. Riley seemed anxious to get going, eyes on the woods all around, and finally his energy infected William and he tossed his blanket off and got to his feet. Kat stirred beneath her bag and released a doleful yawn.

They were a mile or so farther down the trail by eight o'clock that morning, when they stopped to apply more

Vaseline and band-aids to Kat's feet. Calluses were already developing and their concerns about blisters had faded, but he was taking no chances. It was then that they heard voices, coming from behind them. A low growl commenced in Riley's throat. William gripped her mouth with one hand and collected his things with the other. Kat was already moving away with her things on her back. He pulled Riley after her, into the woods, and to cover.

Moments later a man and a woman came into view on the trail. Young people. The man was being supported by the woman, his arm over her shoulder. He appeared to be injured in some way as he staggered while she struggled to hold him steady and keep him moving. She was crying. "You can't," William heard her say. The man seemed to want to lie down as he slowly bent further and further forward. Then down he went, slipping from her grasp. She sighed loudly, ripped off her small backpack and kneeled over him. "Oh, Robert."

William touched Kat arm and gave her a sign to stay. Allowing Riley to follow him, he hurried out to check on the pair.

The woman screamed when she looked up and saw William and the dog hastening toward her. She stood up and pulled a hunting knife from a sheath at her side. Her face trembled with fear. Riley ran ahead of William and toward the woman, but shied away from her when she saw the knife.

William stopped, then walked slowly toward the woman with his hands open in front of his chest. "Maybe I can help."

Her whole body now shook from fear, perhaps fatigue, or perhaps both. The man rolled onto his back and his eyes turned to William. Sweat coated his pale face.

The woman swallowed hard. "How?"

"What's wrong with him?"

"It's…his leg. It's infected."

"Fever?"

"Yes."

William bent forward and examined the man more closely. His shirt and pants were stained with what looked like dried vomit. Blood encircled a hole the size of a dime just below the knee. "I have some medicines," he said to the woman. "Show me?"

The woman's face had also gone pale. Her breath came rapid and shallow. She rolled up the man's pantleg, revealing a three-inch lateral gash, red and swollen and oozing puss.

"Just you two out here?" William asked.

She nodded, a little reluctantly.

"Let's get him out of the sun," said William. "If that's okay with you."

She nodded again and put her knife away—that too, it seemed, a little reluctantly.

"Okay," said William. "You guys are scared. Don't be." He reached down to help the man up. The woman joined him. "That oak over there...can you make it?"

The man nodded as he wobbled to his feet.

They laid him in the deep shade and William jogged over to where Kat sat with their gear, Riley following. He picked up his pack and blanket. "Come with me," he told the girl. "Bring your things."

William gave the man a double dose of antibiotics and a double dose of ibuprofen for the fever. "This will take a while to kick in. Hours, I mean. What's your name?"

"Robert."

"Is this your wife?"

"Yes."

"That's a nasty infection, Robert, and I know you feel like hell, but I think the antibiotics will knock it out."

"Okay." He dropped his head back onto the dead leaves. William spread his blanket nearby and helped him roll onto it.

"What's your name?" William asked the woman.

She noticed Kat coming her way with the dog and gear and seemed to instantly lose some of her anxiety.

William smiled. "Yeah, we're a harmless trio."

114

"Samantha. Sam," the woman said as she knelt beside her husband and stroked his hair. "It's been getting worse. The fever worries me most."

"I think that will spike soon," said William. "He's young. He can fight this. What happened?"

She looked up at William. "They shot him. We were running away but they shot at us anyway."

"They. They still after you?"

"No. They would have caught us if they were. That was two days ago, in Lampe. We've been hiding since."

"Bikers?"

"Yeah. Are you two new here?"

"Pretty much."

"They have some kind of...organization. They have houses here and there with most of the food and weapons from around here."

"We've seen them."

Sam sat down beside Robert and set her hand on his shoulder. "I could kill those bastards."

Kat tossed her gear against the tree trunk and stepped up beside William. "I'm Kat," she said.

"Hi, Kat," said the woman. "You have a dog. Still alive."

"Yeah. I know some people eat dogs. But we take care of her."

"She's lucky. Or smart."

Kat nodded. "We're from down by Ponca."

"I don't know that town."

"It's in Arkansas. We lived under a bridge for a while. Now we're going to my aunt's in Reeds Spring."

"Well, I know Reeds Spring. We have two people from there."

"There are more of you?" William asked.

"Seven, total. Robert and I are trying to get back to our camp."

6

William learned from the couple that the initial EMP attack on the country had affected Missouri as much as it had Arkansas. The social disruption that followed was apparently no less severe. Food was short, well-armed gangs took possession of everything they saw as valuable or useful, and the army and national guard had abandoned their peace-keeping role and had gone home. No one was bringing in any kinds of supplies anymore. All communications had been out from the start. People who knew how to get their vehicles moving again may have left, getting at least as far as their gas would take them, but they were probably robbed and killed soon after. It was doomsday all over the Midwest and probably beyond.

"Your camp," William asked Sam, "how far is it?"

"About three more miles. At least a mile off the trail, though."

"Food is short?"

"It's getting there. We took over one house from the gang in Lampe and got a lot there. That was a couple of weeks ago. But they came back a day later with more people and guns and chased us out. One of us was killed. Beth."

Sam's eyes watered. She wiped at them with her fingers.

"Same story in Arkansas," said William. "I'll leave it at that."

After a while, Robert began shivering and William pulled the sides of the blanket over his body. "It may get worse for a bit. But the fever should break soon."

"Kat," he said, "bring our water jug."

They got as much water into Robert as he could take, spilling a fair amount under the influence of the shakes.

"Some of your people are from Reeds Spring, you said?" William asked Sam.

"Two."

"They ever talk about a hidden shelter or compound in that area?"

Sam looked surprised. "Yes. Pete. He was with a group up there for a while."

"He mention anyone named Linda?"

"Linda. No, I don't think so. He said he left the compound because he had a falling out with the leader. I don't remember the leader's name, but I'm sure it was a man."

William looked at Kat, who listened with rapt attention. "Can you tell us anything else about Linda's place?" he asked her.

Kat shrugged. "Her last name is Gordon. Same as mine and my dad's. That's all I know."

Sam shook her head. "Maybe Pete can tell you more."

7

Sam left them under the oak and went ahead to her camp to bring back help. A few hours later, she returned with two guys and a woman. Pete, Joe, and Sharonne. Joe and Sharonne were in Sam's age range—late twenties. Pete was in his fifties and was apparently the father of another camp member. They brought food and water with them. And a rifle. Pete felt he wasn't of much use and almost immediately returned to their camp, citing other business, and giving William no time to query him.

The rest of them spent the remainder of that day and a whole night under the oak tree waiting for Robert to recover enough to make the hike. He held up well on that hike and when they arrived at the camp his wife introduced Kat and William to the other members of what they called Camp Twain, a collection of four wigwams. Kevin, Sharonne's husband and Pete's son, had been a professor of anthropology at Missouri State in Springfield. He designed the structures.

At a fire that evening, Sam gave William, Kat, and the others the details of what had happened in Lampe. Joe had been out scouting and had seen all the bikes ride out of town the night before. It looked like they were leaving their storehouse unguarded, probably on the assumption that the forest people wouldn't dare another takeover. Or perhaps the prospective raid was just too appealing for anyone to miss out on. Joe reported back and Robert and Sam had volunteered to check it out more closely. They took two of the four guns they had, a pistol, with them. Even before they got close to the house, however, they came under fire and Robert was wounded. In the hasty retreat, Robert lost the pistol.

"Unfortunately, we need whatever they have in that house," Pete said. "We're down to one month's worth of food now."

"We've got our own," William said. "No need to feed us."

Pete waved that off. "We have to try again. I sent Jim out to have another look and to try to find Sam and Robert. He should be back any time."

"We didn't see anyone else on the trail," William said.

"Jim probably took a different route. We have several. He knows them all and a few more of his own."

About eight o'clock, Jim showed up. He reported that all bikes were still absent from the house, but that he saw at least one guy moving around outside. There might be more inside.

"They are cocky bastards," Joe put in. "It would be like them to leave only one or two behind. They sure don't seem to have any fear of us."

"They mostly men?" William asked.

"We count ten men and six women," said Pete. "Every damn one of them can shoot. And twelve bikes."

"You can try to lure them out," said William. "If it's only men in the house, I'd try using a woman."

Several of the group looked around at each other.

"Can you give us more details?" said Pete.

"A woman who would appear to pose no threat. She'd simply walk down the street in front of the house, wearing something skimpy and sexy, and would collapse. How long will they resist the urge to check her out? Longer the better, really. The longer she lies there, the less suspicious they become."

"Damn risky," said Pete. "Simple, but kind of elegant, too."

"Who would volunteer for that?" asked Joe.

"How desperate are you?" William replied.

8

William insisted on going with them. His extra gun would be needed.

They left at midnight: four men and one woman, Sam. She was plenty attractive and had prepared cutoff jeans and donned a thin blouse with no bra. They would position themselves under cover of darkness, close enough to the front of the target house to give themselves a good chance of hitting whatever they might shoot at. The rifle was almost a sure thing to hit its mark. After that, it would be pistols and the results not so certain.

A robust moon in the low western sky lit the scene. The neighborhood was residential. All the houses anywhere near the storehouse had been burned out, no doubt to clear a field of fire and to eliminate cover for any attackers, which meant the bikers weren't completely stupid, or cocky. It also meant the Camp Twain people, and William, had to find less than ideal positions. William lay low behind a red maple across the street and a little west of the house. Its 18-inch diameter was foot short of what he would have liked, but it appeared to be the best he could do if he was to have any chance of hitting anything. He was not a good shot, and his weapon, although powerful, was no sure thing outside of twenty yards.

The other ambushers took up positions somewhere to William's left, spaced, he assumed, to provide different shooting angles but all facing the front of the house. The rifleman was somewhere behind William. His shot was most critical.

Sam's cue was the little hand on her watch at six, the big hand at twelve, about 30 minutes after first daylight arrived. She came out looking convincing, clothes and skin smudged, hair tossed, feeble in bearing. William loved the look on her face—bedraggled and pained were good words for it. Presumably, someone in the house was on watch. William checked with his conscience briefly, to make sure he was willing to kill one of these guys. The image of Matt in his mind settled the issue quickly.

Sam tottered on the street directly in front of the house, then went down, again convincingly, with a loud moan thrown in to awaken any dozing guard. William hoped she hadn't hurt herself. Within seconds, the front door opened. A pistol and two tattooed arms emerged, paused and took aim in various directions. A face with a brown beard and a head with a bandana wrap came next, then the whole body: heavy-set, a big target, clothed in as much leather as the moron could buy or steal.

After a few steps toward the street, the man stopped and turned to look back at the house.

"You crazy?" someone yelled out the door.

The outside guy pointed. "You don't see what I see?"

A second later the inside guy was outside, standing in front of the doorway. Two seconds after that, he dropped onto his face as the sound of a gunshot ripped the morning air.

The first man took a few seconds to grasp what had happened, as did William. The man turned to run for the house when William stood up, took aim, and fired several shots. He thought he heard others fire, as well.

The guy groaned and fell, grabbed at his back and kicked his legs. Then he went still.

Somewhere in all that, Sam had picked herself up and run for cover behind an old doghouse lying on its side not far from William. He waved at her to stay down, which she did.

Suddenly, several shots came from the house. Bullets smacked into the trees where one or more of the Twain people were hiding. It was clear evidence that the assumption of only one or two watchmen was optimistic.

Someone on William's side of the street and behind him opened fire on the doorway, chinking off bits of frame. Return fire from the doorway marked the Twain shooter's position, a pile of weathered lumber.

The occupant, or occupants, maintained the kind of barrage that would come from an automatic rifle, all of it aimed in the vicinity of the woodpile. Not really thinking, William ran for the closest side of the house and slid in behind its wall. He paused for a moment, wondering why he hadn't been shot at. Wasting no more time, he then hurried to the back of the house. He tried the handle on the door there and it opened into a kitchen, unoccupied. He stepped as quietly as he could over the linoleum floor, pistol forward, pointing the weapon from side to side and then at the open doorway to the front of the house.

More firing from the front of the house. A bullet clipped the refrigerator door handle beside William and busted out a back window. Friendly or enemy fire?

He backed against the intervening wall and urged himself to start thinking. *What the fuck am I doing? Does it even matter?*

The shooting stopped. He heard what sounded like the reloading of a clip. Then he heard hurried footsteps advancing toward the kitchen doorway. A second later, a man charged in and swung behind the wall where William stood. Not a foot from William, a guy in camo with a string of teardrop tattoos down his cheek was staring right into William's eyes. A face dripping sweat, pallid, rifle at his side.

William raised his pistol and shot the man under the jaw, right where it met the neck. He dropped hard, here one second, gone the next.

Blood ran in a torrent over the floor. William found himself paralyzed, trying to make sense of what had happened and whether it was real. After a few deep breaths, he listened for more from the front of the house. He heard nothing.

He waited longer. A damn long time. Nothing seemed to be happening inside the house or out.

Finally, he took a quick peek out the kitchen doorway. He thought he had probably seen nothing of concern but wasn't positive. He waited.

"William!" someone finally shouted from outside.

What the fuck was he supposed to do, holler back?

Then he came to his senses. He bolted out the backdoor, turned right the way he had come in, and ran for whatever cover he could find.

Only he couldn't find any. Just the scant remains of a burned-out house.

"Here!" someone shouted from across the street. He ran for the trees there. And he made it. Gasping, heart pounding like a steam engine. Pete was there, sharing a tree with him.

"What happened?" Pete asked.

William couldn't find any words yet; he just shook his head.

"Did you get him?"

William nodded. "I got one. Just one."

Pete stared at the house. "That might be it."

9

No one was willing to advance on the house. Everyone remained behind cover. A couple of shots at the house did not raise any shots in return. William's revving mind and body slowly came under some control. His pistol shook in his hand, nonetheless, and he set it down beside him, his back against the tree trunk.

"We gotta do something," Pete said, taking quick glances at the house. "Oh, shit," he said, his eyes drawn onto the street.

William followed Pete's gaze and saw Sam walking in plain view toward the house. She bent down and picked up the pistol dropped by the big dead man, then suddenly burst into a run and through the doorway.

"Jesus," said William.

They waited, but heard nothing for a good minute. Sam then emerged, waving them forward, raising her arms in a triumphant gesture.

Chapter 10

1

THAT EVENING, back at Camp Twain, the group held a little celebration. Two bottles of wine were retrieved from the storehouse along with frozen meats, cases of canned vegetables, bags of potato chips, and enough turkey jerky and Slim-Jims to raise everyone's blood pressure 10,000 points. Condiments, smoked fish, cereal, and powdered milk. Flashlights and batteries, several guns and ammo, various items of hardware and tools. Too much to carry back in one trip. Four of the attackers spent that many hours conveying the haul from town to a stash in the woods. William had gone back to the camp to round up more help. Much of the haul was yet to be brought in.

There was a lot to talk about and re-live while the newly acquired meats roasted and smoked nearby. No one seemed the least bit upset about the killing of the bikers. Sam was downright gratified. "They shot at me, they nearly killed my husband. Good riddance."

Everyone got a little buzz out of the wine. William was honored with thanks from all involved. When asked why he charged the house, he answered that it was Sam who charged the house, he just snuck in the back door like any real coward would do.

They invited William and Kat to stay on. They would build them their own wigwam. He answered that he and Kat would have to discuss it, but on first blush it seemed a very good and generous offer.

Later, after dark, and after William had a private conversation with Pete, he and Kat laid out their bedding under a dogwood tree and had that discussion.

"What about my aunt?" she asked.

He had to be completely honest with her now. "Kat, most likely their compound didn't make it. Everything would have to go just right for that to happen. Too many things could easily go wrong. That doesn't mean your aunt isn't okay. She may have found another way to make it. Pete tells me—"

Her face went crosswise. "Why do you tell me that now? We were going there together. I thought you would like it there."

"Could be I would, if it's there. But we have a better option now."

"Staying here? I don't know these people."

"They are good people. I promise you that. In my estimation, they are the safest bet. You don't know what the people will be like in Reeds Spring."

"Just because Pete's from there doesn't mean he knows shit."

"Kat—"

"Really. He doesn't know my aunt."

"You said yourself that she could be mean."

"Only sometimes."

Kat flopped down on her leaf-bed. Riley came to her, but she pushed him away.

"Pete was not part of your aunt's compound, but he did hear something about hers," William said. "It wasn't the worst news, but he said they were having some problems. People went there but were turned away, a few of them shot at. Gangs were also closing in on the town.

"You'll be much safer here," William continued after a moment. "At least for now. I've changed our plan. I'm going to go up there myself to check it out. If all is well, I'll come back for you."

"Oh, just great." She crawled into her bag, pulled it over her head, and began to sob.

William stepped closer to her but knew to keep his distance from an upset teenager. "We can talk about it again in the morning. Just give it some thought tonight."

2

"Anything more you can tell me about what to expect on the way?" William asked Pete early the next morning while Kat slept.

They sat around the coals of a small fire drinking coffee, which was the best-tasting coffee William ever had, given he hadn't had any at all for nearly a month.

Pete had already gifted him a hand-drawn map carefully modeled from one of the published maps they needed to hold onto. William stuffed it into his shirt pocket.

"You seem to have the right idea," Pete said. "Stay off the highways and be careful even on the forest roads. The bridge is your main problem."

"Bottleneck?"

"Exactly. They've kept eyes on it. Not always. Less now than before, when there were more people around, more travelers. But be damn sure before you try to cross it. No way off, once you're on it. And even if you get across, Kimberling City on the other side gives you no bypass option. You'll have to make your way right through town. At night, of course."

"Bridge is too high for a water escape?"

"Oh yeah. That jump? It'll finish you."

"You guys gonna be okay with keeping the kid?"

"Sure. Love to have her. I like her spunk."

"I guess that's one word for it. I plan to come back for her. You offer me any estimate of my chances?"

Pete stared down at the coals and shook his head. "Jeez. Who knows? I would say your odds of finding that compound intact are something less than you not getting killed. If I were you, I wouldn't do it. How disappointed can she be? Kids get over stuff like that in no time."

"Yeah, I've considered that, too. It's irrational to try a stunt like that. To be honest, I'm borderline on the idea.

Whatever is pushing me, I don't understand myself. It's more emotional, I think, than rational."

"I kinda know the feeling. We've seen a lot of shit go down lately. It's thrown all of us off."

William drained his coffee mug. "I've been borderline on the whole idea of going ahead with life, period, to be honest again."

Pete nodded. "I get that."

"Could be I just like the feel of making this journey more than the idea of it. A purpose. A sense of control, instead of just waiting around for something lethal to drop down on me. Who knows, maybe the idea does make sense, if it turns out to be the best thing for the girl."

Pete's head came up as he turned to look past William. William turned and saw Kat approaching, wiping sleep from her eyes.

"You ever had coffee?" William asked her.

"'Course," she said as she stepped up to them. "Are we leaving today?"

3

William managed to keep Kat and himself busy with chores all day, including one trip back to the stash to help bring in more of the loot. He had a nap midday. It was a sunny and hot day and the shade didn't cool things much, but he got in a couple of fitful hours.

He had Sam invite Kat and Riley to sleep in her hut that night, coaxing her with promises of a game or two of checkers. That went well, and once Kat was asleep, William finished packing. The added food from the house raid took care of one of his big concerns. A new sleeping bag for him as well. Two smaller water containers that fit nicely into the pockets of his backpack. New flashlight batteries. Even a small pair of birding glasses to replace the ones he had lost back in Arkansas. They would help him scout the bridge. Pete had offered him an automatic rifle, but that was too much to carry.

Pete walked him to the trail. "This moon will help tonight," he said. "A week from now, it'll be dark as hell in these woods."

They shook hands. "Take care of her," William said, and then he started off.

Chapter 11

1

FROM THE HILLTOP, the bridge was plain to see in the moonlight, but glassing it proved to be of little help. The damn thing was huge, narrow but a half-mile long considering it spanned a man-made lake. On the other side, William could see moonlight reflecting off the roofs of buildings, with a darker gap down the middle, which would be the roadway.

This would be like running a gauntlet. If he could run like he used to, that might be the way to do it. Since that wasn't the case, his options were to wait for daylight and employ the glasses, then wait for the next night and assume nothing had changed, or he could blindly go for it even if he had to walk all the way. He chose to wait.

He couldn't read his watch during the night but putting off sleep allowed him to estimate the time, which by his reckoning was two or three o'clock when he began to feel the urgency to do something. It was the lack of sound during that long wait that finally convinced him the coast was likely clear. Voices and certainly engine noise of any kind would have carried across that stretch of water. He gathered his things and made his way through woods and down the hill to the road. Once on the road, it was a long walk further downhill to the bridge. On the way, he passed close by what looked like a retirement community. People had come here to enjoy their remaining years boating and fishing on a cozy lake, having barbeques and cocktails with friends in the park. There was probably a tennis court and swimming pool and a gym somewhere in that cluster of condos. He guessed the complex had escaped total destruction simply because it had made such an easy target.

Once at the bridge, he saw no point in trying to be discrete about it. Discretion on a bridge would be like dressing up for a beer bash. Just had to be quick and certain. Cocky.

He saw no glow of fires on the far side of the lake. No movements except for the flashes of moonlight off the ripples of water below. The pattern of arching steel supports looming over his head made him feel like a gullible animal staring into a trap. He opted to move quickly despite the thought that it might be more noticeable.

The bridge had no walkway, but he kept well to the side and tried to maintain a low profile. About a third of the way across, he stopped and knelt beside the concrete railing and looked ahead to see if anything had changed. There might still be time to retreat if necessary.

After a few minutes he resumed the crossing. The buildings and signs on the other side grew larger and more distinct. Still mostly grey shadows, but the outlines were clear.

Past the halfway point he quickened his pace. The vulnerability of his situation took hold inside him. His heart rate jumped another level and all his senses seemed to sharpen. Something like mania suddenly came on and his head went a little dizzy.

"Screw this," he whispered.

But he kept on. Past the mania, until the end was in clear sight. He ran for it then, if running was what you called the quick leg action of an aging body. The steel supports sloped downward on both sides. The bridge pavement ended at a distinct line under his feet where the road began. He hurried into a lone patch of bushes off the right side of the road. There was a lot of open ground around him there, while up the hill a big-box store of some kind sprawled along the highway, possibly a grocery store. Between him and the store was a patch of woods growing on a steep slope beside the road. He lay low for a while, waiting for anyone's approach, the yelling of a watchful sentry. But there was nothing.

His heart rate and breathing remained full throttle. He checked the holster that the Camp Twain people had given him for his .357. He decided to pull the gun, just in case.

2

William had no frigging way to assess the best route through town. Pistol in hand, he scurried from the bushes and into the woods, where the going was some of the most difficult he had encountered anywhere. Dense growth in front, the highway to his left and an impossible drop-off at his right, had him in a squeeze.

From the woods, he hurried for the side of the big store but felt totally exposed by moonlight there. Instead, he veered across the road to a small strip mall and around the back and hunkered between a pair of dumpsters. If anyone this side of St. Louis was still awake, they'd surely witnessed that pathetic effort at stealth.

After some minutes, he was still alive, and he opted once again for action over thinking. He stood up and moved slowly down the alleyway behind the mall, creeping from wall to junk pile to bush—anywhere the moon didn't light him up. The alley abruptly came to an end when it opened into a parking lot that extended all the way to the highway out front. Across the broad street he made out what was left of a hardware store sign. Probably totally ransacked inside. One of the windows was broken out, its shards scattered in front, reflecting the moonlight.

Directly across the parking lot from him was a peculiar building with what looked like a small steeple over the doorway. Most likely a church. They tended to make their churches in his part of the world look like anything but. Something deceptive about that religion, from buildings to teachings. Well, out of the shadows he went, into the lot, and at that instant he heard something behind him. He stopped. He turned, saw three figures step out of a doorway. Armed men. Guns pointed at his chest.

"Drop the gun," two of them said in unison.

William froze for a moment. The reality of his situation was slow to dawn on him. Then his hand let go of his pistol. One of the men picked up the pistol and belted it. The others backed him against a wall, faces close to his.

"We let 'em cross," one of them said, "then we let 'em scurry around like mice for a while before we nab 'em." The guy was trying to sound like a gangster from a *film noir*. Not a bad impression.

All three were dressed in common clothes, button-up shirts and khakis. One grabbed William's shirt at the shoulder and pulled him away from the wall and held him while another stripped off his backpack and searched his pockets. "Any more weapons?" the searcher said as he pulled William's knife from its sheath.

William shook his head. "You got them all."

The three led him directly across the parking lot to the door with the steeple.

Inside the building, William saw to his left a glass door with "Church Office" in white letters. Ahead was a spacious room that had probably held pews at one time. They hauled him in there.

In the back of the room, a running generator sprouted cable and wires in various directions. It powered a small light on a table where two more men sat in green upholstered chairs on either side of the light. Against the side walls lay a large number of mattresses with sleeping bags, pillows, and blankets strewn over them.

One of the men who had brought him in carried a chair and set it in front of the two sitting by the lamp. The others then dragged William over and sat him in the chair. Now this was definitely like something from a gangster movie.

One of the sitting men smiled at him. "Who are you? Where did you come from? Where are you going?" he asked in a gruff but oddly nonintimidating voice, and as though he had asked those questions many times before.

"Name's William. Came up from Arkansas. Heading to Reeds Spring."

The smiler widened his grin. He was a big man, in his forties, not so tall but quite heavy. Just the type to be the leader of a criminal gang. "Well, I don't blame you for wanting to get out of Arkansas. Why would you go there in the first place?" He laughed.

William shrugged, then said, "I'm willing to admit my mistakes."

A laugh from the big guy again. "I like that." He turned to the other guy sitting with him.

The other guy was much thinner and perhaps taller and was roughly the same age as the big one. He looked sleepy. He wiped at his eyes and drank from a can of Coke. "Mistakes I get," the thin one said. "Mistakes are things smart people do occasionally. Stupidity is something else."

Big laugh from the big guy.

"Although I understand the desire to cross the border," the thin guy said, "the bridge was highly questionable. And you picked a hell of a time to do it. You woke us up."

"Yeah," said Mr. Big. "We could shoot you for that." He laughed again.

"We had him in our sights from the minute he stepped on the bridge," one of the street thugs said over William's shoulder.

"We have night-vision shit here," said Mr. Big. "And other fancy shit."

"So, why Reeds Spring?" Mr. Thin asked.

William straightened in his chair. "Good God. The reason for that eludes even me. I heard of a compound up there. I had nothing else to do."

"We have us an honest man here, I think," said Mr. Big. He fake-punched Mr. Thin on his shoulder.

"Got to be more to it than that," said Mr. Thin. "I don't even understand how you got this far. I would say that's so unlikely it threatens your story. You better give us more." He took another sip of Coke.

"Any chance I could get one of those?" William said, pointing to the can.

Giggle from Mr. Big.

Mr. Thin waved to one of his thugs and the man walked toward the entrance that led to the church office. "Hungry, too?" Mr. Thin asked William.

William shook his head. "Brought plenty with me. Although I guess I won't be seeing it anymore."

"Most we get in here ain't like you," said Mr. Big. "Most shake in their boots or piss themselves."

"I pissed before the bridge," William said.

More laughter from Mr. Big. Another poke at Mr. Thin. "You believe this guy?" Mr. Big said.

"Sounds like someone with nothing to lose," said Mr. Thin. "What's your name again?"

"William."

"Mine's Gil." He pointed. "This guy is Brian, but we call him Ozark." Gil bent forward a little toward William. "I need to hear more from you than jokes, William. We get spies in here, now and then. Saboteurs."

William tried to take in the whole meaning in that. "From where? Who?"

"Gangs. Mostly out of Arkansas. They want what we have."

"I see. I believe I've encountered a few of those guys."

"You must have. How did you get past them?"

"Luck. Staying off the roads. Traveling at night."

Gil nodded. "Luck helps. Any help from other people?"

"No one I care to talk about. I won't lie to you. I had help. But who and where are off-limits."

Ozark giggled again. "Who's in charge here, Mister?" He looked to Gil.

The man who went for the Coke came in and handed it to William. It was cold.

"Cold pop. You people aren't doing too bad here." William opened the can and drank. "Wow, that's good."

"No snitching on friends, then," said Gil. "Why not?"

"I don't know you."

"We don't know you."

"Yeah," Ozark put in. "And we're holding the guns."

William took another drink. "All I will say is that they are good people. No threat to you."

"Who's good and who's bad depends on which side you are on," Gil said.

Gil looked up at one of the men standing behind William. "Put him in jail, Dobs."

"With the woman?" the man replied.

"Why not? They have a lot in common. Besides, I think she can handle him if he gets out of line."

3

The jail was an old auto-repair garage a hundred feet or so from the church. Cattle fencing lined the interiors of the exhaust-blackened stone walls, as well as serving as the "bars" for the one-car entrance, aided by a padlock. It had the oil and gas smell of every other garage William had ever been in.

A mattress and blanket occupied one corner of the cell, a Home Depot five-gallon bucket sat in another. Light came from overhead, a bulb, which the man called Dobs had turned on from the outside by connecting a wire to a surge protector and cable that must have run all the way from the inside generator.

The other occupant of the cell was a senior woman, perhaps in her late sixties. Thin build, long gray hair tied into a pony tail. Not bad looking, even without makeup. She wore faded jeans and a woven cotton blouse with embroidered flowers. Upon seeing William being shoved into the cell, she had backed off. William heard the lock snap shut behind him.

"Sorry about this," he said to the woman. "Not my idea."

She glared out at Dobs. "Is this really necessary?"

Dobs chuckled and walked away. William heard something scrape through the gravel outside. He looked and saw Dobs setting up a recliner chair in the gravel lot.

"I'll be out here," Dobs said. "Awake. And I have a gun."

William looked around the interior but saw nothing else but a bale of hay against one of the walls. No idea what that was for. He heard footsteps approach. "Sleep tight," Dobs said, unplugging the light. Footsteps retreated, accompanied by a snicker.

"It sucks here," the woman said. She walked to the mattress and sat down, back against the wall. In the moonlight reflected from outside, William could just make out the basics of her face.

"Yeah, not the Ritz," William answered. "My name's William. I'm the new prisoner."

"You don't sound local. You give me any news about what's going on out there?"

"I'm a retiree from Minnesota. Not the best decision of my life. As for "out there," well, it's bad. But I suppose it was bad when they dumped you in here."

"Bad but not hopeless. I'm not so sure, now."

William paced the walls, inspecting the segments of cattle fence and tugging on them. They were bolted into the wall with clamps.

"The problem," she said, "is that even if you escape, you go out empty-handed. No food, no weapon. How long do you last?"

He stepped up to the entrance gate and gave *that* a tug, then fingered the lock.

"Nope," she said. "Our best chance is to talk our way out."

"Doesn't look like you've been successful so far," he said.

"I haven't told them what they want to hear yet. And I haven't even figured out what that is exactly."

"How long have you been here?"

"Two weeks. Just my bad luck that the week before they caught a real spy, someone sent from one of the road gangs east of here in Branson. Their suspicion level is high right now."

"They treated you okay? No beatings? Food and water?"

"Food and water when you ask for it. Usually. No rough stuff, as long as you don't consider locking a person up in a place like this "rough.""

"Looks rough to me." He sat against the wall and grabbed his knees. "They took everything I had. And it was a lot."

"How'd you manage to acquire a lot of anything?"

"Ah, well, that's not information I'm prepared to give out just yet."

"Must be why they put you in here, then. If they think you are holding something back, they'll wait you out."

"That true in your case?"

She nodded, smiled.

"I don't know that it would make any difference if I did tell them what they want to know," William said. "But I would need to be sure about that."

"Protecting people?"

"Yeah." He chuckled.

"It just occurred to me," he said after a moment, "that you might be a plant, part of the setup to get information out of me."

"I could say the same to you."

He chuckled again. "Looks like it's going to be pretty quiet in here, then."

4

"You never told me your name," William said after a while. Silence between them wasn't going to work.

She now lay on her back, her knees up, hands behind her head.

"My name is not one of my secrets," she said. "It's Ellen."

"Ah, good. Happy to meet you, Ellen."

She coughed a few times and patted her chest. "You said you were from Minnesota. I had relatives there, in Stillwater. I visited a couple of times, once in winter, once in summer. Two very different experiences."

"Oh, yeah. I lived upstate, north of St. Cloud. A good state for making a living and for making friends. Not so good for retirement. Seven months of cold."

"What's the capital of that state?"

"St. Paul."

"What's the name of the river that runs through Stillwater?"

He gave her a look that she couldn't see. "Well, that would be the St. Croix. And north of Stillwater on that river is Taylors Falls. Quaint spot. Nice ice-cream shop they have there. Homemade. They call the part of the state that borders on Lake Superior the North Shore. North of there you have the BWCA, short for Boundary Waters Canoe Area. The pro hockey team is the Wild. They play in the Excel Center in St. Paul."

"Okay." She giggled. "You pass the trick test. Of course, you could be a plant who happens to actually be from Minnesota."

"Hard to be certain about anything. All you can do is work with the probabilities.

"You must have some really, really important secrets," William went on. "National security stuff, no doubt."

She sat up and looked in his direction. "I'm being a jerk," she said. "Sorry. And no, it's not that important. Just people I don't want to get hurt. Like you, apparently."

He nodded. "I came up here from Arkansas and had trouble on the way, as you might imagine. Some people helped me out. I don't want to give them away."

"Really? Same here. Only I didn't come from Arkansas. I'm from West Plains, originally. Missouri. I was traveling through this area when the trouble broke out. I was lucky and ran into the right people who had a plan. Saved my butt, thank you."

He waited for the rest.

"It's a great hideout. No chance you're getting any more than that from me."

He laughed. "I'll stay clear of that subject, promise."

5

He tried sleeping on the concrete floor with his head pillowed on his arm, but soon realized that sleeping like that was going to de-segment his vertebrae. He got up and walked over to Ellen's mattress.

She was still awake and recoiled slightly when he drew close.

"Here's the deal," he said. "If I don't get some sleep, I will probably spill the beans to these guys tomorrow in a fit of exhaustion. And I cannot sleep on concrete. Back issues."

He waited for a reply.

"And?" she finally said.

He pointed. "It's a queen. Big enough for two."

She hesitated, then squirmed over to give him more room. "Try anything, buster, and I'll tell the warden." She laughed.

"Oh, don't worry. I'm gay." He laid down, his back to her.

"Sure you are."

6

Ellen was up, sitting on the hay bale and reading, when William awoke. A blanched form of sunlight leached in off the street. His watch read seven o'clock.

"What time do they call us for breakfast?" he asked Ellen.

"You don't want to wait for food. You best go back to sleep and let time pass quickly."

He sat up and stroked his three-week-old beard. "Think I'll shower and shave after we eat."

"No, I get the bathroom first."

"Speaking of which. That bucket over there?"

"That's it. Nothing I haven't seen before."

He walked over to the bucket and stared down into it, then positioned himself for a little privacy. It appeared she had already had her bathroom visit. He added to the contents, zipped his fly, then set the bucket into the front corner of the garage opposite the lock. He looked outside to see if he could catch sight of their jailer. He saw the recliner, but no Dobs.

"He says he'll be out there all night," said Ellen, "but after an hour or so, he disappears till morning. Sometimes he comes back drunk."

"Boss won't like that."

"Boss has this whole thing figured out, believe me. Gil's a sharp one. A clever manipulator. But, as far as I can tell, he's not one for brutality."

"What happened to that Branson spy they caught last week?"

"Hello in there!" someone shouted from outside. "It's execution time!"

It sounded like Dobs. Perhaps drunk. The man laughed. "Yeah! I'm here to *execute*...my duties!" Again, he laughed, a little louder.

"Funny, Dobs!" Ellen yelled back.

Ellen walked up to the entrance and stood beside William. She looked up at him. "You're taller than I thought," she said. "Six-two?"

"Close enough."

She looked him over head to toe. "Two hundred even?"

"Close again. Two hundred five when I left home. I'd guess I've dropped about ten."

Dobs staggered up, smelling of booze. He carried a paper bag and a half-gallon jug of clear liquid.

"That water, Dobs, or more vodka?" Ellen said.

"No vodka for jailbirds like you." He handed William the bag, squeezed the jug through one of the fence openings for Ellen, then walked away in the direction he had come and out of sight from the cell.

"Well," said Ellen, "this is something new. I wasn't kidding about having to ask for it."

"We haven't seen what's in the bag yet," William said. He handed it to her and they walked over to the haybale and sat.

The bag contained slices of provolone cheese, four pieces of sourdough bread, and two apples.

"Damn," said Ellen. "You must have connections."

"Not the usual fare?"

"Not even."

They ate the bread and cheese and put the apples back in the bag for later. They continued to sit side by side on the bale.

"The spy last week?" Ellen said. "They told me they shot him. I believed them at first, until I came around to the theory that they were only trying to scare me. That theory has held so far."

"Glad to hear it. But do they ever let you out?"

She nodded. "Yeah. Quite often, actually. Always chaperoned. Like taking a dog out on a leash."

"What I don't get is: what kind of information do they think we have? I doubt they see us as spies. And not being from around here, about all I could tell them is what route I took."

"Hmm, they might think we could be spies. If it had been one of the road gangs that caught us, they would torture us until we told them where to find our hideouts."

William sat quietly for a moment, then walked over to the gate. "Hey, Dobs! I need a mattress!"

Ellen hurried over to him. "A good one!" she yelled to Dobs.

7

An hour later, Dobs showed up. He opened the lock, then the gate. "Let's talk," he said. "Follow me."

Dobs led them back to the gang's sleeping quarters in the church. Gil and Ozark sat in their chairs. Gil was sipping another Coke, like nothing had changed from the night before. Two seats stood in front of Gil and Ozark. Dobs gestured for William and Ellen to take them, which they did.

"You guys still hungry?" said Gil. "We have more if you want it."

"No thanks," said William.

"Well, okay, here's the thing," said Gil. "I want to spare you two any more of the shenanigans and get down to business. I believe you said it well, William. We can't be certain about anything. We have to play the probabilities. So, I want to make you an offer."

William and Ellen exchanged looks.

"I did say that," William said. "How do you know I said it?"

"Dobson there has never had a drink in his life," said Gil. "Right, Dobs?"

William and Ellen both turned to look behind them. Dobs had a big smile on his face.

"I swear on my mother's grave," said Dobs, raising a hand. "Although I have no idea where that might be."

"While you were talking in your cell, he was stone cold sober and listening from another room," said Gil.

Ozark busted out laughing. Even Gil cracked a smile. "Not the absentee drunk you took him for," Gil said.

William took that in but wasn't sure he could digest it.

"This thing has a peculiar odor to it," Ellen said. "Why the sudden change?"

"Simple," Gil replied. "I like what Dobs heard. Your reasons for keeping information from me. I'll buy it."

William and Ellen looked at each other again.

"What I'm saying," Gil went on, "is that I'm satisfied that you two are not spies. You are free. Although I do want to talk business with you."

William stood up slowly in front of his chair. No one moved to restrain him. "And freedom includes getting our things back?"

"Absolutely."

"Okay, let's hear your offer." He looked at Ellen. "Okay with you?"

Ellen stared at Gil. "Gil, this isn't a twisted joke, I hope. You kept me in that little jail of yours for two goddamn weeks."

"You got the same food we got," Ozark put in. "You got the best mattress, too."

"That sure made a difference," Ellen said cynically.

"Yeah, but you were a hard one to figure," Gil said. "To be honest, I thought it likely you were sent here."

"So, adding me to the mix got her to open up," William said.

Gil nodded. Ozark giggled.

William walked behind his chair and up to Dobs. He pulled a quarter from his pants pocket, which, for whatever reason, he hadn't yet thrown away, and handed it to Dobs. "I'd like a Coke. And one for the lady."

Okark shook from head to toe with a big man's laughter.

"Oh, thank you," said Ellen.

Dobs smiled, flipped and caught the coin, and walked off.

William sat back down, although not without fighting back a restless energy inside. "Okay, so what's the deal?"

"Here's the long and the short," Gil said. He placed his hands on his knees. "We need your help. We have unfriendly gangs north, south, and east. We have more gas and food than all of them put together. We have medicines. We have night goggles. And they want all of that. And they are closing in, combining forces. We had three skirmishes with them in the last week. You two have connections with better groups of people, and, from what I gathered from your conversations, they are nearby and have resources. We want to link up."

"Why would they want to?" Ellen asked.

"We're willing to share what we have, but only with the right people."

"You believe that?" William asked Ellen.

She took a moment, then nodded. "Not too crazy an idea."

"Where did you get all the gas and food?" William asked Gil.

"Hah," said Ozark. "My uncle Bernie owns a marina. This town's full of marinas. He knew where the gas was. Them marinas had tons of it. We got it, man." He patted himself on the back and laughed.

"We had trucks bringing food in for weeks before the EMP hit," said Gil. "I was a state senator here before all this. I had some insider information, you might say, on what might be coming."

"Got any more, about what kind of help might be coming from outside?" William asked.

"I do not. Information is as hard to come by now as t-bone steaks."

Dobs entered the room with the Cokes and handed them to Ellen and William. They popped the tops and drank.

"It's the fizz I missed most," William said.

Ellen held her can out for what seemed like a celebratory toast. They touched cans.

"The only problem I see with any of this," William said, "is in the long view. You want people to trust you, to risk their lives, for resources that are going to run out within months, a year or two at best, unless help arrives from outside."

"There's your reason," Gil said. "It might. Probabilities. We're betting on you two, and on help coming."

"Those might both be longshots."

Gil nodded. "There's one more thing: we have seeds. Corn, tomatoes, three types of beans, wheat, and oats. We have a store of potatoes."

"And beets," Ozark said.

"Ready to plant next spring," said Gil. "That's an indefinite supply of food. An expanding supply." He sat back in his chair. "And the gangs want that, too."

8

William and Ellen sat on a shaded bench at the lakeshore, their gear arrayed in front of them. The sun had been up for hours and was pushing the temperature toward ninety, by William's reckoning. The air had gone stagnant as the humidity rose. From the town behind them, they heard voices from time to time as men and women began organizing for the day's projects.

"You met some of the women this morning?" William asked.

"I did. A vigorous bunch. They seem really into this survival thing."

"Well, survival is all we have, our sole shared ambition."

"Amen."

"At times I doubt the sense of it, though, especially for myself."

"An age thing?"

"Yeah. People my age get illnesses. No doctors or hospitals around these days to fix them."

"We have a doctor. She's great. And she brought quite a supply of medicines with her."

"Really. So where is this clan of yours, if I am allowed to ask now?"

"I think I should take you there. I think someone there might have answers for you about the Reeds Spring camp. After that, I'll go with you to your clan, as you call it."

"Ha, I had kind of given up on the Reeds Spring mission, with all this new stuff going on."

"My group is only a few miles from Reeds Spring."

William stood up. "Let's walk a bit, before it gets too hot."

She joined him and they strolled along an asphalt path that followed the shore. "We should have brought our shorts with us," he said.

Ellen looked at the water lapping lightly onto the thin strand of beach. "There's always skinny dipping." She laughed and took his arm in hers.

Chapter 12

1

ONCE OUTSIDE the national forest, Gil had warned them, they would lose their armed escort of Kimberling men. Gil had given them a crude map outlining the backroads and trails they should follow north, but even those would encounter plenty of isolated houses and farms. Mainly, they would have to rely on their own judgment. Ellen seemed little concerned about it. In the presence of their escort, she said only that she would get them there. To William, that kind of confidence from a woman like her was reassuring.

The escort came to a sudden halt after an uneventful six- or seven-mile hike. One of the Kimberling men pointed ahead to an open area—what looked like an overgrown pasture. "Take that direction," he said. He swept his finger about twenty degrees to the right. "There's a farm house over that way. We saw people there about two weeks ago." He handed William his automatic rifle. "The boss said you might not take it. I think you better."

William weighed the thing in his hands. "Never liked toting these things around."

Ellen took it from him. "I have."

The escort headed home. "I'll miss them," William said.

Ellen laughed. "Follow me."

Instead of taking the route advised by the escort, she veered sharply left, avoiding the clearing altogether. "I've been this way before," she explained.

Keeping to the cover of the woods, they reached a dry creek bed after a few hundred yards. From there, Ellen led them north. It was a winding route but was sheltered from view by trees and brush on both sides. Here and there a pool of water oozed up from below the gravel beds on which they walked. William took advantage and wet his face and arms to cut the heat.

The creek crossed a narrow gravel road about two miles along their route. Ellen turned them right, onto the road. She had been quiet most of the way, he supposed because she was keeping an eye out for their safety. He allowed his own attention to wander a bit. She was sixty-seven, but their swim had shown him a shapely female body and practically unblemished skin. The sight of her figure in front of him on this hike revived some old urges. He and Marian had not been very sexually active for years, prior to her death. It hadn't bothered him especially. His reduced sex drive he found to be a new form of freedom. His mind had more time to explore other aspects of life, and it allowed him to claim that he had always been faithful in marriage.

Ellen soon broke from the road and led them back into woods. He could make out minor indications of a lightly used trail—scuffed leaves, broken sticks, trampled raspberry shoots—and then some not so minor: bark shavings on trees, particularly a large mulberry.

"Looks like you know where you're going," he said.

"I do," she said in a near whisper. "But it's best to be as quiet as possible."

Further on, after they climbed and descended a steep hill, they stopped for water and rest. They sat on the roots of a huge sycamore at the edge of another dry creek.

"From here on, we could run into someone from my camp," Ellen said in normal voice. "It's not far now."

"Fantastic. You made that almost easy."

"I am worried, though. Herc, one of the main guys in camp, is not your most open-minded sort. He has followers, and Ellen, our leader, can't always keep them under control."

"Another Ellen?"

"No. Same one."

That paused William for a moment.

"I see. Did Gil know what he had in his little prison?"

"Oh, no. Not that he had all that much. We are an egalitarian bunch, for the most part. I think they look to me because of my age."

"Oh, I can see more reasons than that."

She passed him the water container. He took a drink, then reached behind him and found a way to stuff it into his pack.

After a quiet moment, Ellen set the gun down and took off her pack. She stood up, turned to face William, and held out her hands. Baffled for a moment, he then rose to his feet and she quickly helped him shed his own pack. She took his hands in hers, stared into his eyes, then reached up and touched his face. "I don't know about you," she said, "but I've had something on my mind all day."

2

Well, that was something, all right, William said to himself when they resumed their journey. He wasn't his best, as he remembered it, but he was able to fumble through. Ellen seemed to enjoy it. That was good enough.

Her compound consisted of a large rural brick home with several earth shelters and various other outbuildings scattered around it, some tucked into the nearby woods. The structures lay at the end of a half-mile driveway off a narrow dirt road. The driveway was gated, but the gate had been open. In any case, the wire fence bordering the property could be easily breached.

Ellen was greeted by four men, eight women, and six children, all surprised and overjoyed at her return. They knew of her capture and had assumed the worst, given her extended absence. She assured them that under the circumstances she had been treated passably well.

Ellen deferred the full telling of her story until evening, when a hunting party was expected to return. The infamous Herc was apparently one of the absentees. Ellen gathered that, in her absence, he had recently been voted the new leader. Trouble of some kind appeared to be in the air.

William took a nap on a blanket beneath a large maple. The heat was almost intolerable despite the shade and the breeze from the woods, but he managed to dip into sleep several times. Ellen was occupied inside the big house, which, William understood, was where the single people lived and where meetings were held. Someone had put a lot of money into the overall setup, the source of which William didn't yet know.

After another brief and semi-delirious sleep, this one full of visions of giant bears and saber-toothed cats chasing him across prehistoric landscapes, Ellen came to wake him up.

"Everyone's gathered," she said. "We'd like you to join us. There's fresh venison and pasta."

He stood up and brushed some dry leaf matter from his clothing. "Are we talking business today or just eating?"

"It's an informal, formal meeting, you might say. Yes, lots of business."

3

There were many mouths to feed. William felt only partially entitled, so ate less than he wanted. He learned that Herc was the big, broad-shouldered guy sitting at the end of the long table, which was actually a collection of smaller tables covered with cloth. Herc wore a cowboy shirt with the sleeves removed, displaying a pair of "big guns" as some of his type might say. Thus, the man's nickname. William thought 'Bubba' might serve as well. Herc seemed to enjoy—better, crave—the attention of the others. He had stories to tell and wanted to be heard. The women seemed much less impressed than the men. A much smaller man sitting across the table from William exhibited facial expressions suggesting he had little taste for Herc's dramatics and bravado. His name was Emmitt.

After a dessert of apple pie, Ellen announced that she had a matter to discuss with the group. She asked the children to go outside, a suggestion they gladly obeyed.

Herc appeared uncomfortable. His eyes scanned the table when Ellen continued speaking. "My friend William, here, has accompanied me to help explain a proposal that we bring for your consideration."

Herc cleared his throat. He got right to the point. "Ellen, while you were gone, I was elected the new president. You'll have to leave the running of meetings to me from now on."

"Yes, I heard that," said Ellen. "Congratulations. I really don't care who runs the meeting. The important thing is what we decide to do about the proposal."

"Sure," said Herc. "As long as the question of leadership is understood."

Ellen nodded. "Just let me know when you want us to introduce the proposal."

"Should we have a new election now?" one of the women asked. "Considering that Ellen is back?" She seemed a little anxious about raising the issue, but determined.

A couple of the other women nodded slightly in agreement, but no one vocalized anything.

"We don't have any kind of rules for that," one of the men said. "What's done is done. Ellen said she has no objection."

Several of the men and a couple of women agreed with nods and "uh-huhs."

"To be honest," said Ellen, "I really don't want the job back. I think my circumstances might change after our vote on the proposal."

"Shit," said Emmitt, though barely audible to William.

"Well, let's hear the proposal, then," said Herc.

4

Ellen laid out the offer made by Gil in a logical form, including what she saw as pros and cons. The pros included more resources and crops for the future and a larger organization of forces to fight off the gangs. Single men and women might also want a larger pool from which to locate suitable partners. The hunting territories would be larger.

The cons were a more complicated governing structure and involvement in a shooting war that they had thus far been mostly spared.

After Ellen's presentation, she asked William to talk about the inclusion of the group from south of Kimberling City.

William pulled his chair closer to the table and straightened his back. "Yeah, well, they are a good bunch of people. They are having their own trouble with the gangs. For now, they have enough resources for several months, but they are looking farther ahead and for more security, just like you are."

"How far south of Kimberling?" Herc asked.

"Several miles. The bridge makes for a kind of natural border between them and the Kimberling City group. My guess is, without knowing it, they have been serving as a kind of buffer between the gangs and Kimberling City."

"The bridge isn't buffer enough?" Herc asked.

"Who knows?"

"I like this idea," one of the women said. "If we can get crop seeds, we can have a future. It doesn't get any better than that."

"I have kids," another woman said. "It's all about the future as far as I'm concerned."

"Let's have a vote, then," said Herc.

"Wait, said one of the guys. "We should let everyone speak who wants to. I'm not too keen about a war, myself, but it's probably coming our way anyhow. Maybe we are stronger now than we will be later."

"I say things are pretty damn good now," said a man sitting next to Herc. "If it ain't broke, don't fix it."

"You guys and your fucking slogans," Emmitt put in, his neck grown red just beneath his jaw. "What, do you *think* in slogans? This is a no-brainer."

"Fuck you," the other man said.

"Let's not get into that," one of the women said. "Let's vote before things descend into a brawl. By the way, I too favor the deal."

"I'll call for the vote," Herc said. "All in favor raise a hand."

Nine hands went up, counting Ellen's.

"Sure," Emmitt muttered.

"Opposed?"

Ten opposed, including Herc, who appeared to lead the votes of the other nine. Only two women were with him.

"This is nonsense," Ellen said. "What is this now, a cult?" She held out her hands. "Save your children for God's sake."

Herc smiled. "It's a democracy. The people have spoken."

5

William and Ellen sat outside on the steps of the big house as evening turned to dusk.

"Any chance another vote could be taken?" William asked.

"Only if a lot of people ask for one."

"Nine isn't enough?"

"Well, it has to be more than those who voted opposed. Usually it takes two or three more than a majority. And the request goes to the president, who makes the call."

"Great."

"Sorry about this, William. I thought we had a good chance. The women voting against it surprised me."

"Smart doesn't always win," he said.

"Stupid wins too often," she replied.

They walked over to the spot where William's blanket was spread and lay down for a while, hand in hand. The breeze was much cooler now, making for a comfortable timeout. The maple leaves overhead twitched and twirled in the purple glow of the day's last sunlight.

"Who do I need to talk to about the Reeds Spring compound?" William asked.

"Oh, yes. That would be Emmitt. I'm pretty sure he mentioned leaving that place just before arriving here. I guess he had connections with both groups."

"I'll look him up. He was one of the few men who voted with us. Does he have any clout with the others?"

"The other men? I very much doubt it. He doesn't hunt with them. He hunts now and then, but alone. He spends most of his time reading, and fishing. Seems like a good guy."

When the air chilled further, they drew the blanket over them. "You know," William said, "I can't sleep on bare ground for long. I didn't have time to prepare my usual leaf bed out here."

"One of these earth shelters is mine. That's a good place for you."

He hugged her. "Sounds great. How are the rates?"

6

In the morning, one of the women directed William down to a small river where she believed Emmitt was fishing. Indeed he was.

"Hello, Emmitt. I don't mean to disturb your fishing, but can I have a brief word?"

Emmitt was using a spinning reel and dragging live bait slowly against the current. "Sure." He reeled in and set his pole down against a log. He sat down on the log himself. "Have a seat."

William complied. He scratched at his beard, something that was becoming a habit now that he had one. "I understand you left a compound up at Reeds Spring. A friend of mine has a relative there, or at least did have. I thought you might know her, or about her."

"What's the name?"

"Linda Gordon."

Emmitt didn't have to think. "I know her." He hesitated a moment, looked William in the eye, then peeled off a chip of the log they sat on and flipped it into the water. "Not to sound like a man with an ax to grind, but she's quite the bitch."

"How do you mean?"

Emmitt rubbed his hands together as he worked at getting the worm slime and dirt off. "She had a major stake in that operation up there. She was a big money contributor. Thought that gave her the right to pick and choose who could stay and who had to go. That was after her boyfriend died. He was the chief guy, in the beginning."

"So, the group as a whole managed to stay together?"

"Last I knew." He pulled a small rag from his belt and used that to wipe his hands. "But they were headed downhill, for sure. She kicked me out a month ago."

"Well, I was thinking of going up there to find this Linda and see if she would have room for her niece, a teenager from Arkansas."

Emmitt shook his head. "To be honest, I would rather take my chances with one of the gangs than with that bunch."

"That's pretty extreme."

"Well, that's how I see it." He shrugged. "Maybe a little exaggerated. Anyway, I can't tell you anything more than what I know and how I saw things."

"Think the kid would be mistreated there?"

"They pay little attention to the kids. And there aren't many left. Linda has orchestrated the removal of almost all families. She regards them as a burden and as unproductive. Again, as I see it."

William took a deep breath and exhaled. "Shit. Well, I guess that doesn't exactly offer encouragement to go there."

"If I have discouraged you, I apologize, but I just might have saved your life as well."

"Trouble getting there?"

"Plenty. The gangs control the roads west of Branson, between here and Reeds."

William nodded. "I appreciate what you've told me." He stood up and shook hands with Emmitt. "Can I ask one more thing?"

"Go ahead."

"The vote today. I suspect you regard the outcome the way Ellen and I do: rigged and stupid."

"Ha. Predictable though. I hope Ellen isn't too upset about it, but she should have known."

"Any chance we could turn that around? Get a revote?"

Emmitt chuckled, then thought for a moment. "Outside of murdering Herc, I guess there is only one option."

"Be interested in hearing it."

He took off his cap and wiped his brow, replaced the cap and stared out at the flowing water. "Put a scare into them. Convince them somehow that the gangs are out to get us."

"Ah...." William patted Emmitt on the shoulder. "Yes, yes...I like it." He looked out at the river, then back to Emmitt. "You have any specific ideas?"

7

Over the next two days, Ellen and William kept their distance from Emmitt in order to avoid any hint of close association. William kept busy by taking on repairs to the roof of one of the outbuildings used for food storage. Working on high, slanted roofs had always unnerved him a bit, but he adjusted to it while on the project. Ellen mostly kept to her house, catching up on various chores she had been putting off even before her capture. Emmitt, they saw only in passing and from a distance.

The next morning, William and Ellen were in her shelter getting ready to join the group for breakfast when they heard the commotion outside. One of the women was first to see the object, strung across the gate at the entrance to the compound. She had hurried back to give the news.

Someone had posted a banner on the gate—a big one, apparently. A white sheet with a Nazi swastika painted on it, along with the words, "Coming Soon." William and Ellen joined in the general reaction of horror and concern. They may even have encouraged it a little. One of Herc's henchmen brought the banner into camp and showed it around.

"I hope this is not someone's idea of a joke," one of the women said. "That would be sick," said another. "What do you think it means?" a man asked. "Someone's going to die, is what it means." "What do you mean?" "The person who did this, when we catch him." "Oh."

"It has to be one of the biker gangs," someone finally said.

"Yeah, I've seen them wearing swastikas. Those fuckheads are proud of them."

Herc took the banner in his hands and held it up to the sunlight for inspection. "If they intend to give us trouble, why warn us?"

"Because they're sick. They enjoy that kind of thing."

"They do torture people when they catch them. This is a kind of torture." "What bothers me is that they were so close, and no one noticed." "We need to post sentries."

Herc tossed the banner to one of his men. "Let's meet after breakfast. But just the council."

8

The council was now composed of Herc and four of his supporters, three men and one woman. William and Ellen grabbed a couple of her books and sat in a pair of Adirondack chairs in front of her shelter, awaiting further developments. They spotted Emmitt milling around the big house for a while, then later, as he headed down to his fishing hole with his tackle.

Several men went into the woods with rifles. Ellen suspected they would knock around in there most of the day, looking for any tracks or other clues that might lead to something. Mostly, they just wanted to demonstrate that they were "Real Men of Action."

"Hope he didn't leave any," William said.

"Any what?" Ellen asked.

"Clues."

She chuckled. "He didn't sign it. Anything else isn't going to point to a specific person."

"They've been meeting for quite a while. I wonder if you should join them. Maybe we look *too* distant from this."

She hesitated. "Well, if I barge in there, they might see that as too much concern."

"A delicate game we play here, madam."

"Indeed."

9

The decision was to post sentries, day and night, on a rotating basis. And "everyone was to be vigilant at all times," and to "take nothing for granted," whatever that meant.

The next morning there was nothing to report. No further incidents. Two hunting parties went out, one composed of men, the other of women only—a sort of weekly tradition. Apparently, both were after game this time, not mysterious clues. Several of the other women brought in fresh wildflowers for the interior of the big house. Emmitt played chess on the porch of the house with another man. Others went about whatever daily activities appealed to them, or they thought were necessary.

William and Ellen cut sod from a sunlit flat along the stream and used it to patch her roof. It wasn't really necessary to patch the roof, but it was necessary to appear to be going about a normal life in the community. Ellen invited a few people over for a game of monopoly that afternoon, which they played outside until the rain hit. They finished it inside, relying on everyone's "best recollection" of how many houses and hotels they had on each of their properties. Lots and laughing and storytelling carried them until supper.

The women's hunting party arrived in time for supper. The men's came in around dusk, dirty and tired. They had stopped to cook and eat a possum they had shot but were still hungry and a little pissed that the cook, a nice woman named Jan, hadn't kept food on the table. She went back to the kitchen to make them some peanut butter sandwiches.

It was almost midnight by William's watch when he heard a muffled scream from a distance outside Ellen's shelter. They both climbed from bed and pulled on pants and hurried into the compound's central clearing. Through the big house's windows, they saw beams from flashlights dancing around the interior. They trotted over, opened the door, and stepped inside. People milled about, chattering and waving lights. Several of the beams pointed to the large rear window of the main room, outside of which was a deck and in daylight a scenic view of the woods behind that.

Painted on the window were the words, "AND WE MEAN VERY SOON," bordered with a pattern of small swastikas. One of the house residents had spotted the handiwork while going to the kitchen for a midnight snack.

"Two things I don't like about this," Herc pronounced. "The fucking sign, and people sneaking food without fucking permission!"

"Come on, Herc, we all do it when we need to," the presumed guilty party said, a pretty young woman named Sean who had a big, hairy boyfriend named Cal standing behind her. "No one's trying to hide anything."

"There's no way anyone could get past the sentries," Herc said as he blinked into one of the light beams accidentally pointed his way.

"Well, it looks like someone did," came a reply.

"Bruce, go check on Terry," Herc said. "Make sure the fucker isn't asleep out there." Bruce headed for the door with his light pointing the way. "And check on Alvin, too!"

"How can a few guys watch everything that might be out there?" someone asked.

"It's impossible," said another. "I did the gate and the north woods from six till ten. That's a lot of area to cover. And, yeah, I got bored and sleepy. I admit it."

Emmitt walked over to the sign and stroked the window. "If it makes any difference," he said, "this was painted from the outside, from the deck, so it could be read from the inside."

That was a brilliant move by Emmitt to deflect any suspicion that might be directed at him.

Herc went to the sliding doors that led to the deck and walked outside. He flashed the deck up and down, side to side, took a stroll around it, then bent down and picked something up. He came back in holding that something where people could see it.

It was the butt of a small cigar. "This is a Swisher Sweet, if I'm not mistaken," Herc said. "It's dry and hasn't been there long. We had rain until ten o'clock." He beamed peoples' faces in a slow semicircle. "Anyone here smoke these?"

Silence from the crowd, which was still growing as people continued to arrive from their shelters. Even children came to investigate.

"Does anyone know anyone who smokes these?" Herc asked, waving the butt in the air and shining his light on it.

"I haven't seen anything like that or even heard of Swishes Sweet," a woman said. "I haven't seen anyone smoking any kind of cigar."

"Where's the old guy?" Herc asked.

"Me?" William said.

"No, not you. George. Where's George?"

"Nothing wakes up George," someone answered. "He'd be in his shack."

"Alright, we're having a council meeting right now," said Herc. "Someone go get George and haul his ass over here."

10

Both sentries were found sleeping and both were brought into the council meeting and, by all reports, were browbeaten first thing and shamed to the full extent possible in a small community of peers. George was sent out to resume watch, with the stern warning to "stay upright or suffer severe consequences."

While the council met, some of the residents of the earth shelters remained in the big house living room to await further outcomes. William and Ellen stayed with them. Ellen kept her cards to herself, wisely issuing no reminders of the proposal she had arrived with. William kept his mouth shut completely, simply listening with feigned concern to the anxieties being expressed around the room. They were very encouraging anxieties.

At close to two o'clock, the council came out of the meeting room. Herc and two others approached William.

"We're putting you under lock and key," Herc said to William.

"What?" William replied.

"That's it. We're locking you up. None of this shit was happening until you got here. Everyone else, we trust."

Ellen got up from her seat and right into Herc's face. "You are doing nothing of the kind. He's been with me almost the whole time. He certainly was today and all night."

"You're partial. Your opinion doesn't count here."

"What does partial have to do with it? The facts are the facts. He has a solid alibi. And he doesn't smoke."

Herc motioned to a couple of his guys to take hold of William.

"Give me a break," William said as he stood up and pushed the guys' hands away. "I can walk on my own, sheriff," he said to Herc.

From his locked shed, William could hear yelling going on inside the big house. Ellen's voice was distinct. "You're turning this place into a fascist stalag." "You have lost control and you're just looking for someone to pin the blame on." "Grow up, you turd, and stop jack-booting around here like you think you're some kind of Idi Amin."

Just after dawn, which William could easily view from between the gaping planks of the shed, the lock rattled and the door creaked open. "I guess it's some kind of house arrest," Cal said as he stood by the open door. "Over at Ellen's."

11

While William had been staring with a strange mix of amusement and apprehension at the dark split-cedar walls of a woodshed, Herc and his crew had rummaged through Ellen's pad, looking for Swisher Sweets. From there they went on to other shelters and buildings, and presumably the single rooms in the big house. No one seemed happy about these intrusions, and as the day wore on and nothing resembling a cigar was found, people began gathering in small, animated groups and voicing opinions probably not heard before in this compound. William watched all this from the open doorway of Ellen's home, with Cal standing beside him as the official guard for the day.

Ellen stayed out of these conversations unless asked to join to answer this or that question.

It was late afternoon, after Ellen had retired to her bed for a nap, when two group members—one woman named Joanie and her husband, Erik, who was a member of the council—came to talk with Ellen. Ellen got up and met with them inside, where William, unavoidably, would hear everything said.

"We would like to hear your proposal again, Ellen," Joanie said. "We think a new vote might be a good idea."

12

The new vote that evening came out fifteen in favor and four against. The same count held for the re-election of Ellen to president, even though she reiterated her desire to do other things. "Things were better before," was, in short, the consensus.

Herc did not take this development well. He threatened to leave the compound and take all his weapons with him—a sizeable arsenal, based on his description—but was talked out of it by his closest allies who themselves didn't want to leave.

William was released, not entirely due to reduced suspicion, but because he would be leaving anyway to escort Emmitt to Kimberly City, then moving on to Arkansas and the job of arranging alliances there. Ellen had recommended Emmitt as the group's emissary to Kimberling City. The vote was unanimous—mostly, William believed, because no one else wanted to go. Nevertheless, other than Herc, they all seemed to regard the mission seriously and offered sincere encouragements to Emmitt.

Time had been lost as a result of the initial decision to reject the proposal, and due to the subsequent drama, so William had to get going. His parting from Ellen was the downside of the business, and she clearly shared his feelings, but she was fully behind it. She made him a map of the route south to Kimberling City, the same route they had taken coming north. Emmitt had hunted down that way a few times so he would be another aid.

They hugged, kissed, and said their "good-byes" under a setting sun, promising to get together again as soon as matters were settled.

Not far down the darkening trail, William asked Emmitt where he got the Swisher Sweet.

"Oh, that," he said. "I've got a box of them. I keep them hidden near one of my fishing holes. When I'm down there after dark, I sometimes light one up. Didn't want to share with anybody."

Chapter 13

1

Emmitt's flashlight led them down road, creek bed, and trail until Emmitt felt they were near the town. They waited for dawn in a patch of walnut trees that had one time long ago been planted in rows. Daylight revealed a smattering of burnt and vandalized houses in their vicinity, suggesting the northern reaches of Kimberling City. William's recollection from having walked through the city once before was that it was more small town than city, perhaps holding a few thousand people in all, and most of those on or near the bluff that overlooked the lake. The commercial area was basically limited to the highway that ran through south to north—the highway with the bridge William had formed such an emotional attachment to.

They moved along residential back streets and across neglected lawns and through tiny patches of woods, and, rather clumsily, over chain link fences. Soon the lake came into view through the trees ahead and far below the bluff top. It was then that a burst of gunfire down that way stopped them in their tracks. They ran for cover behind a tin-walled garage.

Each of them carried an automatic rifle and three clips. Each loaded his rifle and flipped off the safety, while the gunfire continued.

Not being the targets of the shooting, they agreed to just wait it out and stay out of the way of stray bullets until things quieted down.

Through a window of the garage, and through another window in the far side of the garage, William saw an assemblage of motorcycles parked in a backyard. He counted six.

"Emmitt, we might be on the wrong side of this fight," William said.

"What do you mean?"

"My guess is bikers up ahead, probably shooting down the hill at the people we came here to help."

"How can you be sure?"

William pointed Emmitt to the window, and the man rose and had a look for himself. "Uh-huh, good guess," Emmitt said as he dropped back down.

They were both quiet for a time. The shooting came in spurts, intense for a few moments, then fading into longer silences, then picking up again.

"How badly do you want to help these people?" Emmitt asked.

William had no specific answer to that. "Shit. It's why we came. There is a lot hanging on this."

"That's true. Enough to get killed for?"

William sat back against the garage wall. He turned the gun over in his hands and inspected its mechanical design, its engineering. A tool of death, no doubt. Some saw beauty in it; he saw only that tool of death. Meanwhile, his mind raced in a circle.

"I suggest we try to bluff them," William finally said.

"Better than attacking, I suppose," Emmitt replied. "But what kind of bluff do you have in mind?"

"Fire our weapons a few times, then tell them they're surrounded, and to throw down their guns and beat it."

"That sounds a bit Hollywood to me. What if they refuse?"

"They don't know it's only two of us. Why wouldn't they believe it?"

Emmitt hesitated. "I agree, they *should* believe it, but in my experience these guys are a full marathon away from smart. They will come for their bikes, which are sitting practically in our laps."

"Won't matter, if they have disposed of their guns."

Emmitt was quiet. A lot to think about. William didn't press it. Meanwhile, another mad burst of gunfire rocked the air from below.

"Fuck it," Emmitt said. "You got something you want to live for bad enough, take off. I won't blame you. I'll take care of this here."

"What? No way."

Another moment of silence passed.

"Okay," William said, raising his rifle. "I'm about to cut loose. You're the one they need to get these two groups together. *You* take off."

Emmitt rose up beside William. "So, who does the talking?"

"Me," William replied. He put his rifle on automatic, pointed it into the trees ahead, and pulled the trigger. Emmitt's rifle kicked in with his.

2

Sometime during William's and Emmitt's two-man fusillade, the shooting ahead of them had stopped. Both emptied their clip and replaced it.

"Hey, fuckers!" William yelled. "Drop your guns and get the fuck out of here or we close in on you! No one gets out alive!"

No answer.

"Last chance!"

Still no answer. Then, "Fuck you!" from below and bullets ripped through the vegetation and into the buildings around William and Emmitt.

"We better shoot back," said Emmitt. And they did, a couple of short bursts.

Again, the shooting from below ceased. William shouted, "All right. Do it, or we'll torch your bikes. I got the matches and gas in hand."

Another few moments of silence, then, "Fuck it! How do we know you won't shoot?"

"You don't, asshole! But we damn sure will after we've burned your bikes and have to come down there for you."

A minute later, several figures emerged from behind the ruins of a house, hands in the air. They wore all the typical biker garb, but there were no weapons in sight. Five men, not six.

William and Emmitt held their guns on target as the bikers approached directly, then angled toward their bikes.

"Good so far!" William yelled at them. "One wrong move...." The Hollywood silliness of his speech was not lost on William, but what else should he say? Better to just keep his mouth shut.

The bikers passed by, no more than twenty yards away, eyes darting between their bikes and the men holding rifles on them. Another man rushed out from behind the ruined house and William instinctively swung around and fired at him. Everyone ducked.

"Fuck!" one of the first group of bikers yelled. "We're going!" William turned back to the sixth biker, saw him lying on the ground and waving his hands. "Unarmed!" he screamed.

Emmitt gestured the man forward to join his buddies. They all climbed on their bikes and roared away, a couple of them flipping off William and Emmitt as they disappeared around a curve in the road.

"You're not much of a shot, are you?" said Emmitt.

William shook himself out of whatever mystical trance state he had been operating under for the past few minutes. He smiled at Emmitt. Emmitt laughed out loud. "Never said I was," William said. "Let's get their guns and beat it."

3

The Kimberling City defenders wouldn't come in close after William had called out to them. Nor would they buy his story of captured weapons and retreating bikers, even though they had heard the bikes leaving. They never heard the name 'William' and doubted he was any kind of associate of their boss, Gil. They told William and Emmitt to "scram."

William suggested they send a runner to Gil to get his identity verified. They yelled back that would be a waste of time. "Identity, horseshit!" one of them added.

"What about Ellen?" William shouted. "She was your prisoner! She's a friend of ours!"

"You mean that spy we had locked up?"

"What the hell, don't you people talk to one another?"

No response.

"Okay," William said, "I'll come down unarmed! How's that? I'll walk you back to see the load of guns up here!"

"Load of shit, more like it!"

William turned to Emmitt and questioned him with a look.

"Hey, these are your people," Emmitt said. "They're not going to listen to me."

"We are going to leave these guns right here, then!" William yelled. "Tell Gil that we will walk down the middle of Highway 13 in two hours, unarmed! He can meet us in the road or at his church!"

There was no response to that either. William led Emmitt away from the weapons pile, back to the north for a quarter mile or so, then to the east where they would cut the highway at some point. A street named James River Road took them to that highway. They sat near the intersection to rest and grab some food, a couple of P&B sandwiches the cook, Jan, had sent along. After they had eaten, Emmitt pulled two Swisher Sweets from his pack and offered one to William. "Sure," William said.

4

Gil met them where they had hoped he would, in the middle of the highway well north of his church. Gil apologized for the behavior of his men earlier, saying that good soldiers rarely made good diplomats. He seemed happy to meet Emmitt.

"I'm glad there was no gunfire between you," Gil said. "Nevertheless, we have two wounded from that little skirmish. You probably prevented more. Thank you."

"Never occurred to me to just shoot those bikers on the spot," William said. "Break my pact with them. I guess I'm not such a good soldier either."

Gil shrugged. "Just keep in mind that the next time they won't return the gesture."

Gil looked to Emmitt and took a deep breath. "Give it to me straight, then. Do we have an alliance?"

"We do," Emmitt said, smiling. "A close vote initially, but sound reason prevailed."

William laughed. "A little more to it than that, but all is good. Emmitt will serve as the go-between. He plays chess and reads Bertrand Russell."

Gil chuckled. "Well, then, we are in business."

They walked back to the church and along the way Emmitt and Gil learned that they were both graduates of Missouri State and both had majored in political science, with a few professors in common, even though the enrollment periods differed by a few years. From there Gil had gone to the law school at the University of Missouri, while Emmitt had changed fields and attended graduate school in physics at the University of Illinois. Any kind of positive bonding was great news, and despite the rocky beginning, the alliance seemed likely to succeed.

5

The church nave looked more like a hospital ward, circa 1863 Gettysburg. Gil assured William that most of the people lying on the mattresses, wearing ragged and dirty clothes, were not wounded, just tired, taking their customary afternoon naps. Several were nursing minor injuries from work accidents, and two were victims of the recent shootout. One man caught a bullet in his liver area, the other victim, a woman, had been shot in the foot. The shirtless man with the body wound had been heavily bandaged and given morphine and was unconscious.

"We have a great supply of pharmaceuticals," Gil explained to William and Emmitt, "but not the professional knowledge to go with it. Certainly, no surgeon."

"Maybe we can help with that," said Emmitt. "We have a doctor in our group. Probably not trained in surgery, but I can't say for sure."

"Which one is that?" William asked.

"Sean. Remember her? Mid-thirties, blond, pretty, a little on the robust side."

William remembered. She had a big boyfriend. "Oh, yeah."

"How soon could you get her here?" Gil asked.

Emmitt shrugged. "A matter of hours, not days. Say ten or twelve. I hope she'll come. She's…well…kind of the insecure type. Not exactly a risk-taker."

"We'll give her whatever she wants that we have."

"Worth a try," said Emmitt. "This man's chances aren't good, I take it?"

Gil shook his head. "I doubt even your doctor can save him. You need to tell her that. I want to do whatever we can, but we have to be realistic, too.

"Before you go," Gil went on, "I've prepared a special pack for you to take. It's got some food items your group may not have, and a set of night-vision goggles, military grade. Call it a show of good faith."

Emmitt seemed a little taken aback. He then reached into his own pack, pulled out a Swisher Sweet, and handed it to Gil. "And one for you."

They all three chuckled.

"Didn't mean to be disrespectful here," Emmitt quickly said. "Maybe not the place for humor."

Gil waved it off. "Humor is all we have to deal with this shit sometimes. Feel free. It's *Mash* here 24/7."

While Emmitt shucked his pack and loaded on the new one, Gil waved Ozark over from where he stood waiting. The big man brought a piece of cloth and handed it to Gil.

Gil unfolded the cloth, revealing a symbol, black on white, of what looked like a primitive rendering of the Kimberling Bridge. "Wave this out on the highway when you return." He handed it to Emmitt. "Hopefully no one will shoot at you. And tell your leader I'd like him to set up a meeting for us. I'll come there."

Emmitt smiled. "Our leader is a she. I'll carry the message. See you then." He turned and walked away toward the church entrance. No goodbye or "see you later" for William.

"He's a bit odd," William said in hushed tones to Gil. "But you can count on him.

"Oh," William added. "You remember Ellen?"

"How could I forget?"

"Their leader."

Gil stared at him for a moment. "You mean, our Ellen?"

William nodded with a grin.

"Oh, boy."

6

Gil had a special pack prepared for William as well, presumably with much the same contents as the one given to Emmitt. William didn't ask.

"What's your strength here, Gil?" he asked instead. "Been wondering about that."

Gil gestured around the room. "What you see here is a small part of it. We have fifty-two men and thirty-seven women. They're distributed around the town in five locations. Each has pretty much identical responsibilities. Keeping eyes out for intruders is one, but feeding and sanitary duties and the like...all that."

"Children?"

"Sorry, yes. We have a school, in fact. Two teachers. Sixteen kids."

"What about the bad guys? Any idea of their numbers, locations, etc.?"

Gil led William out of the nave and into the office, where a desk was coated with a scattering of papers and a refrigerator stood defiantly in a corner—source of the Coke, William assumed. Gil noticed the attraction and gestured, "Help yourself. I'll have one, too."

They popped the cans and drank while Gil pulled a map out from under the array of papers and spread it over the top.

"We are here." He made a circular motion to indicate an area around Kimberling City. "Emmitt's people, from what he said, are up here somewhere, not that far from us, leaving a gap. But as near as we can tell, the gangs haven't set up anything permanent in there, yet.

"Here's our bridge, then farther south is your group. I'm guessing in this area, west and maybe north of Lampe. You made it through that gap okay. That surprised me because our scouts have identified a couple of houses in there that the gangs use frequently. They like Highway 13. Made for bikes, in their view. Lots of downhill curves."

"High potential for crashes," said William. "A secret ally."

Gil laughed. "It's happened. Just not enough.

"Anyway, we believe there are four of these road gangs in this part of the state. One in Branson, here, and the one in the Lampe and Blue Eye area. Then one up in Galena, further north. One in Forsythe that's rubbing shoulders with the Branson band, and not always in a friendly way."

"Shit. How many people?"

"Our guess is around three hundred, total. At least a hundred in Branson alone, probably more. The Lampe group seems fairly small, maybe thirty."

"Less than that now," said William. "The Twain Camp knocked off three just before I got here. Walked off with a major cache of their supplies."

"Great news." Gil paused. "I hope they escape retaliation. Let them know we can help."

Chapter 14

1

GIL HAD ASKED for two volunteers to accompany William to Camp Twain. Their names were Jason and Carmen. Jason was a short and stout young man who had scouted the area south of the bridge several times. It was kind of his specialty, William gathered. Carmen was a physical phenomenon, with broad shoulders and narrow hips for a woman. She had muscles where few men had them, and a determined look on her face that said, "Don't mess with me." She didn't need the determined look on her face.

This crossing of the bridge was pleasant, an evening crossing. William took the time to enjoy the cool rise of air off the water and the aquatic odors it carried. A blood-red sunset topped it off. His company led him to a small cabin on the far side where they would sleep well into the night before climbing the long hill pre-dawn, then slide into the forest for concealment. William needed that sleep. It had been a long day for an old man.

2

The only trouble encountered on the hike to Camp Twain was William's less than precise recollection of the route. The trails got confusing with more branches than he remembered. Luckily, Jason's memory was better. His ventures into the area had painted a close estimate of the whereabouts of the camp, based on traffic densities and occasional late-night sounds that often traveled far and wide through the forest. He knew of the main trail into Lampe.

Jason got them close, and close was enough for them to be spotted by Robert, who was on watch near the branch trail that led to camp. He recognized William and emerged like a panther from his camouflaged hideout.

"William!" he said in a relaxed manner, lowering his rifle.

"Hello, Robert. Yes, please don't shoot. We come in peace and bearing gifts."

Robert laughed, shook William's hand. William introduced his company and explained the general reason and nature of the visit.

"That sounds promising," Robert said. "Let's get you to camp and explore it."

3

Kat nearly went out of her mind when she spotted William walking into camp with the others. She was checking laundry that was strung on a rope between two trees. She ran at him without a word, but then leaped onto him, arms around his neck, nearly bringing him down. He dropped his rifle and hugged her.

"Oh, my God!" she screamed. "Oh, my God! Oh, my God!"

"No, just the old man," he answered.

She set her feet on the ground, then jumped on him again. "You old man!" she said. As he held her, she trembled, shook, and finally sank into a sobbing fit.

William held her close as others from camp began to gather, smiles on their faces. Finally, the girl released him, stood quietly and wiped at her eyes.

"Kat, is that really you?" William asked.

"'Course."

"Well, if it is, it's a new you."

"Oh, stop that." She gave him a little shove. "It's me. I still might shoot you one of these days."

He laughed. "That's more like it. But I don't mind this new Kat either. So good to see you. And doing well, it looks like." He glanced at Sam, who was standing near. Those looked like tears in her eyes, as well.

"Oh, man. It's just me," he said. "But I've brought some good news." He saw Pete hurrying over from the vicinity of his wigwam. He waved.

"Well, if it isn't the old dog from Arkansas," Pete said. He shook William's hand. "Please call ahead next time so we can tidy things up a bit."

"I tried, but the line was busy."

Kat came in close and hugged William again. "Riley's going to be happy about this."

"Where is the hound?" he asked.

"Oh, probably hunting squirrels."

"You got a place for me to rest?"

She took his hand. "Yeah. Follow me."

William looked at the others and shrugged. "We'll talk later."

4

It was late afternoon when everyone except Jim, the lookout, was gathered around the main fire. Sam had come to visit with William after Kat had gone back to her laundry duties. "She really did miss you," Sam said, sitting down with William.

"So it appeared. I hadn't seen that side of her before."

"She's been through a lot. Most kids these days are confused and scared pretty much all the time. They could all use some intense counseling. Those still alive. We're lucky, in a way, that none of us have them."

"You the acting counselor for Kat?"

"Ha. Well, I do my share, I guess. Kat was hard at first, but you see how she's adapting. We're glad to have her."

"She mentioned Reeds Spring lately?"

"Oh, that. Not so much lately. She's been reading that book you gave her, *Treasure Island*. It's kept her busy."

"I'll have a talk with her about Reeds Spring. It won't be bad news, but not what she hoped for, either."

Now that they were all gathered, conversations turned to matters of a less personal nature. William explained to the camp the situation in Kimberling City, their proposal to link up in some way, and assured them that the leader up there was trustworthy. He opened the pack sent by Gil and poured out the contents.

"Ooh's" followed, as they saw a full box of Payday bars, smoked meats, packages of mixed nuts, assorted boxes of crackers, and even blocks of cheddar and swiss cheese scattered over the ground. "Damn," someone said when catching sight of the night-vision goggles. Joe reached down and picked them up.

"They're not lacking for resources up there," William said, "but they are surrounded by gangs who want to take it."

"So, what exactly do they want from us?" Pete asked.

"Gil, their leader, is open to ideas at this point. I know he wants your protection from the Lampe gang. They are a threat from the Highway 13 direction. If you could control that highway, then that might be enough. The more damage you can do to that gang, the better."

"We're a small camp, William," Pete said. "It's a struggle to stay afloat. Hard to see how we can go on the offensive."

"They have a lot of support up there in Kimberling, people and guns. I'm sure they would share. This camp would give them a base."

Pete seemed conflicted but said nothing.

"That's how I see it, Pete," said William. "Gil can speak for himself, if you would care to meet."

Pete looked around at the others. His eyes locked on Carmen. "They sure look healthy enough."

General laughter kicked in. Carmen smiled weakly but offered no other response.

"This is something we will have to discuss as a group, by ourselves," Pete said to William. "So everyone can feel free to express themselves."

"I get that. We'll catch up on our rest. Let us know…whenever."

William stood and led Carmen and Jason away.

5

Sharonne carried over plates of food for William, Jason, and Carmen, while the main dinner and discussion proceeded without them. Jason and Carmen seemed to have nothing to say to William, or to each other. They lay down in the grass near William and closed their eyes. When Pete came over with the news, they all sat up.

They had a majority of votes in favor, Pete said, although one wanted to think on it more and discuss it with her husband in private. That would be either Sam or Sharonne, the two married women.

William kept away from all contacts to avoid the appearance of meddling. He expected the majority to win out. He spent the evening reading one of the books Ellen had given him, a mystery set on the coast of Wessex. He wondered for the millionth time whether the rest of the world was in the same situation as the U.S. If not, surely some kind of help would arrive eventually. He had always assumed that it was the Russians who had detonated the high-altitude bombs. Someone, somewhere, knew the answer, but getting it to the public in the Midwest was not yet possible.

He slept well under the dogwood, a bed of leaves for him again, until the shot woke him. One shot, then two in rapid succession, then two more. All close, in camp.

He jumped up and fumbled for his rifle in the dark, found it, and looked around. He heard both hushed and shrill talk coming from some of the wigwams. At the far side of camp, he saw a shadowy figure run toward the branch trail that led to the main. He grabbed a flashlight and ran in that direction, and when he got to the spot where he first saw the figure, he saw two more, two murky outlines, lying on the ground. His light revealed the faces of Pete and Jason. Both shot in the chest and in the head.

Sam, Robert, and all the others except Jim, who was patrolling, joined him.

"Oh, good God," said Sharonne. "Oh, my God!" Her hand went over her mouth.

"Not Pete," Kevin said. He put his arm around his wife and pulled her close.

With his own flashlight, Robert bent down to examine the bodies. "Someone shot them. For fucks sake! Who shot Pete?"

Robert looked up at William.

William couldn't tell if there was accusation in Robert's eyes. "Carmen," he said. "Someone ran off, that way." He pointed. "Carmen is missing."

"Fuck this!" Robert said. "Why?"

William shook his head. His pounding heart seemed to sink in his chest. "I don't know. I really don't know." Behind the ring of people, he saw Kat coming their way. "Sam," he pointed to Kat. Sam looked and immediately ran to Kat, took her by the arm, and led her back to the wigwams.

William checked the safety on his rifle. He started off for the trail, his mind hazy but his blood burning with vengeance.

"Stop!" Robert shouted.

William stopped, turned around.

"William, you're too old. You won't catch her."

The fire in him cooled a little, but only a little. *Think,* he told himself. *Get a grip.*

"We can cut her off," said Joe. "There's a major shortcut. It's dangerous going at night, but it's faster."

Kevin ran off toward Pete's wigwam.

"Fuck," said Robert. "They've got us fucked over."

His own responsibility for this was finally catching up to William. His gut went even further south, bending him over. "Shit," he said. His knees shook. The rifle slipped from his hand and landed at his feet. He couldn't find any words for these people. "I brought her; I have to get her," was all he could say.

He reached down and fumbled with the rifle as he tried to pick it up. "I don't believe you knew about this," someone said as he got a grip on the weapon and raised it.

"God, what a shitty thing," said someone else.

After a moment of silence, Kevin arrived. "The pack is gone," he said. "The one William brought. The goggles with it."

"We won't catch her if we don't get moving," said Joe.

"Nobody's leaving," William said. "Only me. Nobody else is risking their life on this." He started toward the trail.

"Where're you going?" Robert asked.

William looked back as he hurried away. "Lampe. I need to know."

Chapter 15

1

THERE WAS NO POINT in looking for the woman's tracks in faint moonlight and on a trail frequented by the Camp Twain people. All he could do was maintain a pace that wouldn't leave him too far behind but also not burn him out. His heart rate and breathing told him he was probably getting it just about right. Lampe wasn't far. He knew the way now, and Lampe had to be it. No way Gil was behind this. Just no way.

Here and there he spotted familiar landmarks, even in dim light—a tall pine with an overhanging bow, a ridgeline with a deep saddle. The first shapes of buildings emerged in front of him before he anticipated, those outlying homes that were only partially burned. Past them were the ruins of the town itself, already upon him.

He slipped between two of the remaining structures still over ten feet high to where he could get a view of the storehouse. He expected to see the glint of moonlight off motorcycle chrome, but nothing like that came into view. The house was dark. He sat and watched it, aching for some sign of life that might be her.

He was about to make a run for the back of the house again when movement to his left stopped him. He made himself small, as a figure crossed the street near the spot where Sam had crossed some days ago. It was her. No one else had a body like that. His guess: she had been watching the house just as he was, to make sure it was safe to approach.

She stopped at the edge of the yard, raised a hand to her mouth, and whistled. Three sharp notes. No answer from the house. She walked up to the front door with her weapon pointed straight ahead. She shucked the pack she was carrying and eased into the doorway where she stopped again, her figure still visible to William.

He raised his rifle and aimed for her legs. Then he lowered the rifle and made sure the safety was off and the rifle was set on semi-automatic, the setting he always kept it on. He re-aimed, then fired twice.

Down she went. With a scream.

2

He stopped the bleeding with her own top, which he stripped off her bulky shoulders with little concern for her comfort or modesty. She was bra-less beneath. One of the wounds was minor, a two-inch laceration of her right calf. The other was near the left knee, with what looked like bone splinters glazed by moonlight around the wide and dark hole. She was writhing in pain when he had reached her and kicked away her rifle, and while he pressed the wounds closed, and she was still writhing in pain.

He saw the pistol holder at her side and pulled that weapon and belted it. Took her knife as well.

"You got anymore on you?" he asked.

"Fuck you!" she screamed. She lay on her side now, pounding the doorway landing with her fist.

"You're the one who's fucked here," he said. "You can have it either way. I can finish you off, or I can leave you here to die slowly. Your friends aren't coming back."

She said nothing. She groaned and arched upward as if to stand but fell back onto her side.

"You answer my question, and I'll leave you with some morphine," he said. "Otherwise...."

"You...you ain't got no fucking morphine. What, it's in your pocket?"

He had no pack, so she had him there.

"Okay. I suppose option three is that I can make your slow demise even worse." He put his foot on her wounded knee, applied a little pressure. Her head jerked back as she screamed.

"And I can do that kind of thing all night and day," he said. "And I'll enjoy it."

Her breathing got faster and deeper. Her eyes began to roll back but then came straight again. He took his foot off her knee.

"W-What's your question?" she asked finally.

"Actually, more than one. First, who sent you to Kimberling?"

Blood dripped from the woman's nose, which must have struck the concrete landing in her fall. She wiped at it. He took the fingers of her hand and showed her where to pinch her nose to stop the bleeding.

"Who?" he asked again.

"These guys."

"These bikers here?"

"Yeah."

"Why?"

"What? Why not? They wanted to know what those people have up there."

"Oh, shit! Ahhh, it hurts!" she screamed, grabbing her knee.

"Yeah, that's a nasty wound. Likely to get infected."

"What-what more do you want?"

"I want to know why you shot Pete."

"Goddamn!"

"What?"

"He-He was their leader, man. Why do you think?"

William picked up the woman's rifle and started to walk away, then he came back for the pack, set down the two rifles, and heaved the pack onto his back.

"Shit, man!" she said. "Can't you help me?"

He stared down at her. The bleeding from the knee was stopped but the internal damage had to be severe.

"I'll be honest with you," he said. "Unless you have a surgeon handy, nobody can fix that knee. It's going to kill you one way or another.

"Look, I can end it for you quickly, if you want." That's what he said. *But could he? A woman?*

She looked down, propped herself on her elbows, began sobbing, moaning. No reply to his offer.

He picked up the rifles. He wanted to say he was sorry. But for what?

"Maybe…maybe I'll send someone back with some medicine." As he walked away, the moaning and crying followed him.

"Okay!" she cried. "Okay!"

He stopped and turned to look back.

"Finish me! Oh, God!"

3

Dawn came up slowly as William made his way back to Camp Twain. He stopped at several points, fatigued, but also unsure what any of this was about anymore. Where was he going? And why?

He stopped again and sat beside the trail, laid the rifles on the ground. Morning birds began singing deeper in the woods. The dampness in the air hung like a thick soup around him. Seventy-two years of life had not taught him anything about how to deal with the likes of this. Two innocent people dead due to his decisions, his actions. Why couldn't he see it in that woman? He saw something that wasn't right, but he didn't look close enough. He got lazy.

The fatigue hit him like a hammer. He rolled onto his side, the pack going with him. His body shook for a moment, then went stone still, immovable. He tried to raise himself, but nothing wanted to work like it was supposed to. He closed his eyes under the weight of heavy lids and let the world go black, his mind with it.

4

Sam and Robert woke him. They knelt beside him in flickering sunlight that filtered through the trees. A warm breeze moved along the trail. "William, are you okay?" Sam said. She held a water bottle.

He tried to sit up but needed their help. "Ahh, so, you're here," he said, his senses not yet alert.

"Yes," said Sam. "We got worried. Drink. I think you're dehydrated."

He downed a few gulps of water.

"You found the pack," Robert said.

William nodded. He started to get to his feet but his knees buckled. "Yeah. Don't think I can carry it, though."

Robert stripped the pack from William's back and loaded it onto his own. He picked up the extra rifle. "She leave all this?" he asked.

William shook his head. "Doesn't matter." Tears formed in his eyes and his lips trembled, even while he felt little emotion. He drank more water. He gasped for a substantial breath of air. "We can't get Pete back."

"You're exhausted," Sam said, placing her hand on his shoulder. "You've been taxing yourself way too much. Let's get you back to camp. We're all so sorry about Pete, but no one blames you."

They helped him to his feet.

5

William slept under the dogwood the remainder of the day, waking only in brief stretches in which the stares from the camp occupants discouraged any sort of engagement. He dreamt of huge bears in a variety of peculiar shapes, either too long or too wide, heads half human, all intent on pursuing him and tearing him to pieces. Tall trees gave him temporary refuge, but escape came only with wakening. At some point he noticed that his rifle and pistol were gone.

He woke again when Sam shook his shoulder. It was dinner time, she said. The others were all sitting about the cooking fire. "C'mon, William. Please eat with us. I can't keep Kat away from you any longer."

They gave him a plate of food, but his hunger had not yet returned. He managed only to pick at it. Kat sat beside him. "Don't worry," she said. "You don't have to eat if you don't want to. I made the rice myself, but it's not really that good. Sam said I didn't use enough water."

William nodded to her and offered a weak smile.

"William, we are still interested in an alliance, if you still think it's a good idea," Sam said.

William set his plate down on a stone beside his plank bench. "She was one of the Lampe Gang. She was spying for them in Kimberling City. She saw a chance to get rid of your leader and decided to take it. Maybe it was revenge for the raids on their storehouse, or maybe it was part of a bigger plan."

"You caught her, then?" Robert asked.

William nodded. "No one else was at the house. I left her there, wounded."

"You didn't finish her?"

"No."

Everyone was quiet for a moment, exchanging glances. "Why the hell not?" Joe asked.

William shook his head.

"Just because she has tits?" said Joe.

"William," said Sam, "We might need to verify your story."

He looked at them in turn. "Yeah. Makes sense. She's at the house. Not going anywhere. Should be safe."

Jim tossed his empty plate onto the ground, stood, picked up his rifle, and started off.

"It's up to you," William called out to Jim, "but you might want to take along some antibiotics and painkiller. She'll die there without them."

Jim slowed for a second, then continued toward the trail.

6

Kat and William played checkers at the dogwood until sleepiness got the better of her and she lay down and in moments was out. He carried her to Sam's wigwam. "Got something for you here," he said to Sam.

He carried her into her bed, laid her down gently, and covered her with her bag. Sam took him by the arm and led him outside.

"It's only a couple of them who have suspicions," she said. "Robert and I sure don't."

He thanked her. She hugged him.

"We really need this alliance, William. We are so thin now. We'll all be dead by spring."

He nodded. "There's more to the alliance than more people and guns and the rest. They have crop seeds, Sam. All kinds. They have the seeds, but being trapped in that town by hillside woods and lakes and enemy gangs doesn't afford them much suitable land. They need space."

"We have that."

"You do. And there is more to the north. My good friend Ellen leads the neighboring group up that way. They are already working with the Kimberling people."

She took his hand. "They've asked me to take on Pete's role here. I'm no Pete. I could use that kind of help too."

"I can be ready to go by morning," he said.

"Are you sure? You've been pushing yourself so hard."

"Getting used to it now. I feel like I'm sixty again."

They laughed.

7

William grabbed a little more sleep that night and by morning indeed felt ready to get going when he saw Jim walk into camp from the trail. The object he carried in his hand was a belt, which he dropped beside the cooking fire where everyone had come to hear the news. William walked over to join them.

"That's hers," Jim said, pointing to the belt. "She was alive but not going anywhere, today or ever."

"You finished her?" Kevin asked.

Jim nodded. "Happily."

"She have anything to say?" Robert asked.

"Oh, yeah. She asked for painkiller. Said she was forced into the whole thing. She was just a soldier following orders. All that shit. I told her the only painkiller I had with me was a bullet."

"Good," said Robert.

"So," said Sam, "we good with letting William go do his thing?"

People nodded.

"William," she said, "please hurry. The Lampe Gang might try to retaliate."

Kat grabbed William's arm. "Watch your back, old man," she said with a giggle.

He hugged her. "I'll be moving so fast my back will be far out ahead of me."

Chapter 16

1

THE HIKE BACK to Kimberling City was becoming routine. That would be about the time to expect something out of the ordinary to pop up. Which it did, in the form of three parked motorcycles in the place where the trail met Highway 13 at the top of the long downhill slope to the bridge.

William immediately retreated a few yards off the trail and ducked into cover.

There were no other signs of anyone around, but his options were limited. He put his rifle on safety-off, unstrapped his pack, and sat behind a log and a tree trunk to wait it out.

Nearly two hours passed but still nothing.

He made his way toward the bikes cautiously, ears and eyes keened for encounter. The bikes appeared to be perfectly operable. He guessed the riders had left them there to scout the town and didn't want to ride in too close to give the alarm. He pulled his pocket knife and quietly ripped out wires and slit the tires on all three bikes, then slinked back to his hiding place. He had no plan beyond that, other than to enjoy the distress of the bikers when they returned.

Another two hours passed before they showed up, walking into the little turnout area from the downhill stretch of highway. Three men, all carrying rifles, talking quietly. One had an expensive pair of binoculars hanging from his neck. As soon as the men saw the condition of the bikes, the rifles went slack.

"What the fuck!" one of them called out, just short of a scream.

Another pushed him and slapped a hand over his mouth. He raised his rifle and panned the nearby woods, did the same to the woods across the road. William then realized how stupid he had been to stick around this close.

The three spread out and dropped to the ground, into the roadside ditch where William couldn't see them. He curled against his log shield and prayed as only a nonbeliever could that they stayed where they were.

When William was a kid, they called this kind of thing a Mexican Standoff, although he never knew where that term came from. Who would take the chance and make the first move? He decided it would not be him. He heard whispering from the three men and regarded that as a good sign—they weren't moving into the woods.

As time passed without further developments, William felt himself getting sleepy. How in hell could he? His frigging life was at stake. Old age had its own priorities, he supposed. One must be that sleep was more important than staying alive.

Dusk came in. Still occasional whispering near the bikes, some of it sounding as frustrated as he felt. Then, to his surprise, one of the men stood up. William feared he might spray the woods with bullets, but then he realized, as they would, that shooting would probably be heard in town. Instead, the man hurried away on foot, heading south on the highway. Only seconds later, the other two rose up and did the same. The standoff was over.

In the movies, the hero would immediately rush out into the road and say his farewell with a few perfectly directed shots at the retreating enemy. William stayed put. He had waited this long. A person was only a hero if someone was watching who could regard his actions as brave and magnanimous. He doubted the squirrels and possums that might be watching would hold him in such high regard.

When dark finally settled in, such caution seemed excessive. He crawled out and made his way to the bikes. Why he hadn't searched their saddlebags before, brought his rationality back into doubt. It seemed he could never pull off this kind of thing with precision. There was always some misstep. He opened each bag and scooped out its contents and in several trips carried all of it a short distance into the woods, where he pulled out his flashlight and had a look.

Mostly tools, extra shirts, small bottles of engine oil, maps, gloves, cigarettes and matches, and spare clips for the rifles. One item looked interesting. It was a partial roadmap of the area, torn out of a larger one, with several locations circled and numbered. Kimberling City was circled, the number "100" written nearby. An area northwest of Lampe, "10." North of Kimberling and west of Highway 13, "20." Finally, near Reeds Spring, "40." Obviously estimates, not precise. He crammed the map into his pocket, let the remainder of the stuff lie, and set off for town.

2

Gil thought it was a scouting party that had probably visited each of the gangs' target areas to get updated people counts. They were waiting to see some thinning out before mounting a serious assault, was his thinking. That was the reason for the occasional small attacks: to ambush one here, two there. They were making progress on that front. Kimberling had lost six in the last month.

In the nave of the church, the two wounded Kimberling men from the latest fight were doing okay. They thought even the one with the body wound would survive. Sean had come, escorted by Emmitt and a few of the Kimberling group that had gone north with him. She was now a goddess-healer among the Kimberling crowd.

Gil was packing his things for the trip north to meet with Ellen. Emmitt and Sean had preceded him, with escort.

"I need six or seven, Gil." William said. "The people at Lampe are in dire need." He took a drink from his Coke.

"If they're still scouting us, then a major attack seems unlikely," Gil said. "You can have them. Just make sure Celine is one of them."

William then recounted the Carmen incident while Gil selected food items for his pack.

"Shit," said Gil. He set down his pack. "Damn it! I'm sorry. I hope they—"

"They're okay with you. It was a bad hit, but they need you more than ever now."

"Take whoever you need. Let them know they will be there for a while. I'd say two weeks at least. They got enough food down there?"

"Yes. For now."

Gil went back to packing. "I am truly sorry for Carmen. She had us fooled."

William shook his head. "Gotta move on." He tossed a warm can of Coke into Gil's pack. "That going to be enough for you?"

Gil chuckled. "Have to be. Too heavy."

"Tell Ellen that I'm looking forward to seeing her soon. I thought she might be here with you, but I guess she felt she couldn't get away. She has a bit of a thorn in her side. A guy named Herc."

Gil zipped up his pack. "Hah. I know the type. I deal with Ellen only."

3

William asked around the church for volunteers and found three, including the one named Celine. Those three found three more. Three men and three women, total. They all seemed excited about the notion of getting out of town and seeing something new. At the bridge crossing they stopped midway and held a little ceremony, something in honor of a friend who was killed a few weeks before. William kept back, but it sounded like a couple of prayers were spoken. One of them dropped an object of some kind over the side.

When they reached the turnout where the bikes had been abandoned, William was surprised to see them still there. "Oh, they'll come for them," one of his escorts said. Another picked up a nearby rock the size of a human head and did as much damage as he could to the master cylinders, rotors, hand clutches, and voltage regulators of each bike. "They can have them now," he said.

Later, as they approached the cutoff from the main trail to Camp Twain, Joe called out from the woods: "That you, William?"

"Sure is! I've brought company! Good company!"

"Glad to hear it! Go ahead!" Joe sounded like he was up in a tree somewhere, but William never saw him.

Kat came running out to greet him when they reached the wigwams. She had become quite a hugger. He pulled a Milky Way from the side pocket of his khaki pants and gave it to her. He also gave her a Slim-Jim. "For Riley," he said. She turned and called out for the dog, who appeared to have been sleeping in the shade of William's dogwood. Riley came running.

Sam and the others weren't far behind and William spent some time making introductions. "Sam, I guess you are the one to organize everything. These newbies will need some orientation, a couple of wigwams, and whatever else."

"Oh, I have a plan," she said. "We've got the makings of the shelters already cut over in the woods there." She pointed, then addressed the new residents. "It will sure be nice to be able to sleep again without worry. Thank you all so much for coming. And you, William."

4

Each of the escorts had brought a supply of food along, which they shared at dinner. Two fires were now needed for the cooking. One of the new people asked Sam how they dared to make fire. She said they had not had their territory raided for two months, that the Lampe Gang had been hurt each time they came near. Besides, warm food was necessary for morale, she said. "No guarantees, though. There aren't so many of them now, but those left might get desperate."

Celine explained how the Kimberling group suspected the gangs were beginning to work together and were planning a big attack. Celine was a petite middle-aged woman with a cheeky face and shallow dimples, narrow brown eyes, short and spikey brown hair worn like a crown.

"We've been worried about that kind of thing," Sam said.

"Gil has asked these new folks to help secure the highway," William said. "He thought that maybe together you could take over Lampe and move your people in there."

"Interesting idea," Sam said. "The storehouse is intact. And a couple of other structures. But wouldn't we be more vulnerable there? We like to stay clear of the highway. That's bike territory."

"I agree with that," said Celine.

Everyone's eyes turned to Celine. There had to be more.

"Look," Celine went on, her own eyes catching some of the fire. "If they do get help from Branson, the bikers would overrun whatever we had in town. It's a long ride around from Branson to Lampe, and a lot of gas, but if they think it's worth it, they will do it. They will surely do it when they make their big attack. That's the thing we need to prevent."

"If we don't block them in Lampe, then how do we keep them from using the highway?" William asked.

"Simple," Celine said. "We can start on that tomorrow."

"Got dynamite?" William asked jokingly.

Celine smiled and shook her head. "They'd just cut a short bike path through the woods. We'll try something better."

5

Two of the Kimberling detachment to Camp Twain set off into the woods with Jim early the next morning. Jim had told Sam that their intention was to scout the highway. William was a little unclear about what exactly they would be looking for but gathered that it was locations and not bikers. Celine was normally not talkative, but after a private breakfast with Kat, William asked Sam to join him in a meeting with her. They found Celine in the woods stripping bark off saplings to use as bindings for her wigwam.

"In the interest of open communication," William said to Celine, "can you fill us in on the purpose of the scout this morning?"

Celine sheathed her knife. "Oh, yeah." She sighed. "Sorry about that. I'm used to my own way of doing things, I guess." She wiped her sweating face on her shirt sleeve. William reflected on the fact that the women often wore men's shirts because they tended to hold up better in rough conditions. "Yeah, well, I asked the guys to find a few spots we can use for ambushes. That's basically all there is to the plan. Simple, really. We'll keep a strike force out on the highway at all times. Move them around so the bikers can't predict when or where."

"Oh," William said.

Sam smiled. "I like that."

"Three or four shooters should be enough. Well-spaced. It's best to let at least one target get away to spread the word."

"You done this kind of thing before?" William asked.

"No, not quite like this."

Sam and William waited for an explanation.

"Well, it sounds, like you said, simple," said Sam.

"But effective," William added.

Celine nodded and wiped her face again. "How do you folks cool off around here?"

Sam pointed east, then west. "The trails are primitive, but there are lakes on either side, no more than a mile. If that's too far, then we have a creek just north." She pointed again. "That's our water source. Drinking, laundry, and bathing. For bathing, we'd like you downstream a hundred yards or so."

Celine nodded.

"That's all, then?" Celine said.

William looked at Sam. "Guess so," he said.

"Yeah," said Sam. "We'll leave you to your work."

Back at the wigwams, Sam turned to William. "Part of this is going to be getting used to other types."

William laughed. "I've had to do that a lot lately."

6

William corralled the excited Kat, who seemed bent on asking every newcomer what he or she knew about Reeds Spring. He invited her to try fishing at the west lake, and they were at the shore no more than an hour later, each with a stick for a rod and some old line and hooks that William had rediscovered tucked away in his Arkansas backpack.

A sycamore provided shade next to a small finger inlet that William thought might surprise them with a few sunfish. They settled in there, fixed their line and hooks, and baited the hooks with worms that William had tucked away in his pant's side-pocket that morning. They dropped the works into the water.

"So, Kat, you seem happy here with the Twain people. Getting along with everyone?"

"'Course."

"And now you've got some new friends from Kimberling City?"

"Wouldn't call them friends, exactly. They only just got here."

"How about that Tom? He's not much older than you, is he?"

"Way older. He's nineteen."

William bobbed his baited worm about three feet beneath the water's the surface. "Oh. Yeah, I guess that's a lot older."

"I know it's not a lot of years."

"Think he's cute?"

She glared at William. "God!"

William laughed. "Well, then, he must have had a lot to say. You were talking with him half the morning."

She held her stare. "I talked with a lot of people. You're kinda nosey today."

He nodded. "Yes. I can be nosey. But sometimes it pays off. I talked to a guy who told me a little about what been going on at Reeds Spring."

"What is it?"

"Not a lot. But the last he knew was that your aunt's compound was still there, only it was having some trouble holding together. Some people were leaving. There are no children there, now."

"I'm not exactly a child anymore. There aren't children here either."

He thought he had a bite and jerked his pole, but nothing.

"I know," he said. "But from what I've seen and heard, this place here, Kimberling City, and even my friend

Ellen's place farther north, all look like better fits for you than whatever might be in Reeds Spring."

Kat pulled in her bait. Her worm was gone.

"When you feel a tug on your line," he said, "give the pole a little jerk to hook the fish."

"I been fishing before. You need to stop treating me like a kid."

They were quiet for a while.

"Well, I just wanted you to think about your future," William said. "That's a grownup thing to do."

"I do that all the time."

"Yeah?"

After a while, William said, "Sam sure seems to like you. You talk to her much?"

Kat didn't answer right away.

"Sam's my best friend," she finally said. "And maybe that includes you."

He laughed. "Well, it's easy on me, being nothing but that silly old man."

A good twenty minutes passed without a word between them. Then Kat set her pole down and scooted in close to William. She put her arm around him and lay her head against his shoulder. He put his arm around her, and she began sobbing.

Chapter 17

1

JIM AND THE TWO MEMBERS of the scouting party returned to Camp Twain at evening. They had identified three locations for ambushes, one north of Lampe and two south. Celine believed that two or three successful attacks would be enough to dissuade further use of the highway by the gangs. Two squads were formed of four fighters each, including both old and new members of the camp. Each squad would post on the highway for two days before being relieved. After an active ambush, the ambushing squad would immediately return to camp and the other would re-post to another location.

William volunteered as a member of Squad One. Kevin and two of Celine's people, Amanda and a guy called Hammer, made up the rest of the squad. They followed crude maps that Jim had created, showing the three locations, labeled simply A, B, and C. Squad One posted at Ambush A, north of Lampe and a few miles south of the bridge. They built hammocks from rope and cloth, most of which had been stolen from the Lampe storehouse. The sleeping area was set up fifty yards back from the highway and the shooter positions. Shooters were stationed ten yards apart on the same side of the highway. Logs were placed to provide cover, yet still look natural. Each member of the squad chose his own permanent position.

One shooter was always in position while the other three rested or slept, on a rotating basis, with replacement every four hours. Any approaching bikes would be easily heard by all, of course, but having a pair of eyes on the blacktop at all times seemed prudent.

William expected visitors soon. Three bikes were most likely still parked a short distance north of Ambush A. Despite their current condition, their owners would be anxious to recover and repair them. Having left on foot, those owners would be a while getting to wherever they might hitch a ride back with new supplies for the bikes. The situation could get interesting at any moment.

2

William was third in the rotation and went out to his position at midnight after a fitful sleep. Midnight till four a.m. Graveyard shift for the one with snoozing issues. He might want to trade off with one of the others later for a better time slot.

Middle of the night seemed like a ripe time for a visit, under cover of darkness, when forest people would likely be sleeping. On the other hand, these bikers seemed pretty cocky about their dominance of the roadways. In their minds, the forest people would keep to their little green sanctuaries and not dare open warfare against superior forces.

William still had mixed feelings about shooting at people. Self-defense was a noble concept that had been used as an excuse for centuries, probably longer. With all the death and murder that had gone on lately, it could be argued this would be a drop in the bucket, justifiable on many grounds. But there was that instinct, the internal resistance, to not kill something so like yourself. And there might be women among them.

He kept his rifle with its safety on and lying on the ground beside him. He used leaves to soften the ground where he lay, and he had brought his sleeping bag with him in case it got chilly. He lay on his back most of the time, head propped on the bag, occasionally turning his head for a quick look north and south down the road, but mostly it was a matter of ears listening for the unusual. And staying awake.

Stars through the trees above and the time of year promised as much comfort as was possible in the Ozark woods at night. His back felt pretty good and had probably gotten stronger with all the recent activity of his new lifestyle. As he stared at those stars, he wished he could, at least occasionally, be more "in the moment," in the way the Buddhists and his wife Marian encouraged. "At one with the world," as they said. The art of "not thinking." But he always had trouble with that idea. He was a man of thought. He *liked* to think, and to ponder both past and future. That gave depth to living. Merely existing in some disengaged state of consciousness was about the most boring thing he could imagine. Living was all about engagement. Simply "being" was for something else. Who could say what?

3

William checked his watch with his flashlight. Two-twenty. Damn, it was one-ten at his last check and that couldn't have been more than twenty minutes before. He must have fallen asleep after all, without even knowing it was coming on. He sat up and had a look around as he reached to his side and felt his weapon lying there. The moon was higher in the sky, the constellations noticeably shifted westward. But no signs of activity at the earth level. He thought he could hear one of his companions snoring back in the woods.

No damage done, thankfully. Only a little over an hour and a half to go on his watch.

Instead of lying down, he leaned his back against the log shield he had set up and slapped his face a couple of times. He didn't *feel* sleepy. He had to assume that sleep was just something that was going to happen now and then, this time of night, whether he wanted it to or not.

With his kind of active and wandering mind, he found it hard to keep his attention on surroundings, especially in the absence of light, and in almost total silence. He should mention this to the others. Perhaps two-hour shifts would be better.

Only a few moments later, he thought he heard a distant, low-pitch rumble. Faint, but something. When it grew slowly louder, he put his fingers to his lips and whistled. Less than a minute later, the others came rushing through the trees and fell into their positions.

"You hear it?" William asked Hammer.

"Yep."

"Yes, definitely," said Amanda.

"Remember," William said, "if it happens, don't fire on the last in the line if you can help it."

"When do we fire?" Kevin asked. "When they are right in front of us?"

"You get any advice on that from Celine?" William asked Hammer.

"No. I didn't."

"Shoot before they reach us, is my suggestion," said William. "Could be hard to hit them if they are streaking by. How about everyone shoot when I shoot."

All agreed.

The sound was unmistakable at that point, and moments later the light beams scattered over the sky above the road to the south. William checked his safety. "Safeties off," he said. "Careful not to shoot me. I'm close to your line of fire."

"Easy and calm," said Amanda. "Cool as cucumbers. No crazy-ass spray-shooting."

"Aim just above the headlights," Kevin said.

Now those lights were in view. Four that William could see. Then two more, farther back. "They could be riding double," he warned the others.

Those were last words spoken. When the lights reached a spot about forty yards from William, he opened fire on the first bike—five or six shots—then jumped to the next, just to the left of the first. He heard the others firing behind him.

All kinds of mayhem broke loose on the blacktop. Lights went sliding toward the ditches as crashing metal kicked up sparks from the asphalt, and screams, both human and mechanical, tore through the air. Some lights went out. Tall grass and bushes on both sides of the road toppled into unnatural angles in the moonlight as they snapped and groaned along the new paths carved by crashing bikes. William had stopped firing, he realized. He simply watched as the tumbling dark heaps came closer and closer before finally dying amidst the dirt and vegetation of the roadsides. Fifty feet or so behind the wreckage, the last two headlights slowed their approach and peeled away, one to the right and one to the left, off the road, then back on as their tail lights became visible and whatever those things were they were towing bounced and rattled behind them. The bike engines roared in panic back down the blacktop, their taillights disappearing suddenly into a dip or around a curve.

As the sound of bikes faded, moans and cries became audible nearby.

"Finish them off?" Kevin asked from behind William.

William had no answer yet.

Not ten feet from William, the wheels of one of the bikes still spun, its spokes sparkling in the moonlight. Ten feet further back, a body-shadow crawled along the bottom of the ditch. That was one source of the moaning. There were more on the other side of the road.

Hammer didn't debate the issue. He was on his feet, shooting again, automatic rounds struck at anything that moved or made a sound near the road. Cries went silent in no time.

4

William advised they wait to examine the damage. The riders had certainly come armed, and one or two might still be a threat. He and the others kept their distance from one another so as to not present a group target. They stood behind and against trees. Hammer lit a cigarette.

"There's going to be gas out there," William reminded. "All over the place." In fact, he could smell it.

"Three bikes," said Amanda. "Any guess as to how many riders?"

No one had a clue.

"Four bikes down," said Hammer.

After a moment, Amanda agreed. "Right, four."

"Were we lucky or unlucky not to hit the others with a stray bullet?" Kevin asked.

"Well, we hit what we were shooting at," said Hammer.

They waited quietly for about five more minutes, then William took it upon himself to be the first. *Spare the children*, he thought. He flipped on his flashlight and walked out.

The man in the ditch nearby was dead. William saw three obvious bullet wounds to the torso and a lot of abrasions on the face. Not far along in the same ditch, he found a second man. He thought he recognized this one from the bunch he had encountered at the turnout. So, he had been riding passenger to get back to his own bike. The trailers must have been hauling spare tires and other supplies for repairs. Anyway, this one was just as dead as the first. A hit to the forehead had been enough. His brains lay in a small stream behind the opening at the back of his skull.

"Two dead over here," said Hammer from the other side of the road.

"And two here," said William.

Amanda walked a little farther down the road where the third and fourth bikes piled together in the center of the highway. As William went to join her, he heard two quick pops from Amanda's rifle, then another. "Two here," she said.

5

Dawn revealed that one of the bikes was not damaged too badly. Hammer thought that all it needed was a new gas tank. William knew just where he could get one. A bike might come in handy for the Twain Camp.

Hammer also thought it made sense to hang the bodies, five males and one woman, from trees, as a warning to other intruders. William spoke against that. His argument was that some semblance of civility was important to maintain. They decided to drag them into the woods far enough that odors would not be a problem for future ambushers at this site.

The bikes, they also dragged from the road and concealed with brush and logs.

So, that whole experience had gone relatively quickly and smoothly. Already they were headed back to camp, to a warm meal, and, for William at least, a long rest.

Chapter 18

1

WHILE WILLIAM SLEPT most of the day, dreaming of flocks of white birds descending on graveyards and turning into yellow-eyed ravens with the tongues of snakes, much had been going on in the real world as well. Upon awakening, he learned that Squad Two had taken their positions south of Lampe in daylight and within an hour had come under fire. In their case, the bikes numbered close to twenty, many with two riders. They roared down Highway 13 with guns blazing, strafing the woods on both sides for miles, beginning south of where the squad was set up to well north of the town. At least that was how it looked and sounded to the ambushers, who took to cover and wisely did not return fire on the first pass. On the bikers' return, their gunners were mostly quiet, appearing to select targets on a whim. Once they were past the ambush location, Squad Two fired at their backs, knocking down three more bikes. The other bikes kept moving and did not return.

Upon hearing this, William went to see Celine, who was sitting on the ground outside her new wigwam cleaning her rifle. The rifle had seen a lot of action that day.

"So, you got three more?" William said.

She nodded.

William offered her a small can of WD40 that he had used earlier on his own weapon and kept in his cargo pants pocket. She nodded again and put the contents to work at once.

"I think your strategy is brilliant," he told her. "Obviously, it's had great success sooner than we could have hoped."

No reaction from her.

"It also seems obvious that the gangs want that highway open. I thought the one beating would be enough to keep them away. But they came back hard."

He pointed to a spot on the stock of her rifle that looked like dried blood. She rubbed it away.

"I think they will try again," he said. "But I don't think they will try the highway next time. No way they can target us there, thanks to your plan."

"You can skip the flattery," Celine said as she continued to work on her rifle. "I agree with you. They'll come at us here."

William was taken aback a bit. "Oh. Okay. Looks like you are way ahead of the rest of us again."

She shook her head. "Just common sense."

"Well, if...when...they do decide to come, they have a good idea where to find us. Within a mile, anyway."

"What makes you think so?"

"I saw a map they had made. This area was circled as an enemy location."

Celine set her gun down and pulled a half-eaten Payday bar from her shirt pocket and took a bite. "So how do you think they'll do it?" she mumbled.

"Find us?"

"Right."

"First off, the map had an estimate of the number of people in the camp. Their estimates of the other camps and Kimberling were darn accurate. They had us at ten. That was before you guys arrived. But we're not many more than that now. If the Branson Gang is behind this latest bit of action, which I believe it is, then they will think they can simply overpower us. They will be willing to take some losses to be rid of us and to keep that highway open."

"They haven't done it yet."

"No, but that was the Lampe Gang. They didn't have enough people."

Celine smiled, surprisingly, although not making eye contact with William. "You're pretty good for an old guy." She took another bite of her bar and chewed for a moment. "I sent Tom back to Kimberling early this morning for more reinforcements. I hope we can get ten."

2

The stakeouts on Highway 13 were discontinued. In their place, Celine and Sam sent out teams of two to watch the main forest trail south and north, and single sentries east and west in case the bikers tried to approach through the rougher terrain. Everyone had some kind of watch duty on a daily basis. It was not sustainable, which everyone understood, so the hope for reinforcements was the best thing going.

After breakfast, William invited Kat to a game of checkers. She said she had laundry to do, so he helped her with that. Dunk, soap, scrub on rocks, dunk, wring out, dunk, wring out, hang to dry. "I'm due for a change of clothes myself," he said. "Any of my dirties in this pile?"

"They all look the same to me."

"Remember how we did it on the way here?"

She giggled. "'Course. In the river. This is better."

He let some time pass while they worked, then said, "Has Sam talked to you about how to protect yourself if we ever have trouble in camp?"

"Sam? No. And you should stop being so...whatever...gentle with me about that stuff. You don't mean trouble, you mean if we are attacked by the road gangs. I can protect myself. I know how to shoot an automatic rifle."

"Yeah, I've seen you shoot. But anyway, it would be good to have you close by me — or at least, close to Sam."

"Good for who?"

He nodded, laughed. "Good for me, I guess."

"Okay. When the shooting starts, come find me. I'll protect you." She squealed and shook with laughter and splashed him with water from the stream.

3

Tom returned late that evening from Kimberling City with only three more, each with enough food to last him or her for a week. Sam called for a general camp meeting in the central open. The crowd arrayed in a semicircle, some sitting, some standing, with Sam in front.

"Kimberling has asked us to leave camp here and set up a new camp at the head of the bridge," Sam said. "That's so we can defend the bridge more easily when they attack the town. Kimberling thinks the attack will come in a couple of days. They will send us more reinforcements when we're at our new camp." She paused while looking around at the faces of the group. "I, for one, am a little unsure about that idea. We have been safe here so far."

Several of the original camp members agreed, although one added, "But I like the idea of more help."

Small discussions broke out among the members. Then Celine stepped forward and turned to the group.

"A camp is a target," she said. "Even if it is only temporary. We don't have the numbers for that kind of fight. You are not safe here anymore, either. I have another idea."

"The Kimberling people have taken over here!" Joe shouted with some obvious resentment. "This is our camp! We should decide!"

A few heads nodded, but no more voices were raised.

"We are one group now," said Celine. "We aren't Kimberling and you aren't Twain. That's the only way we can win."

William stood up. "I know both. I know you people and I know, and respect, the leaders at Kimberling City. They are good people up there, just like you. You couldn't tell the difference."

"It's hard to move from safe to unsure, William," Sam said. "What you and Celine are saying makes perfect sense, but there are emotional ties here."

"Can you defend this camp against forty or fifty from the gangs?" Celine asked. "They can come from all sides."

"You said you had a better idea," Joe put in. "Well, what is it?"

"It's a lot like what we did the last couple of days. Small groups, spread out, hitting them here, then there. No central base that they can attack, but with the bridge as the main object of defense."

"How would the groups communicate?" William asked, saying the first thing that came to his mind. "We could end up shooting at each other."

Celine appeared stumped by the question. "Good point, William. Look, I haven't thought all of this through yet. We should get our heads together on the details. But as a basic strategy, that's the way I think we should go."

"For how long?" Joe asked. "We can't keep that up for long."

"We can for a few days," said Sam. "A week."

It dawned on William how difficult the coordination would be. Where would the groups camp? Would each have a territory? How would a defense of the bridge actually be coordinated?

"Let's set up a committee to work out the details," William said. "The committee can present the plan to the whole camp."

Everyone seemed to agree with that.

After some discussion and voting, Sam, Celine, Joe, William, and Jim comprised the committee.

4

Coordination proved to be the deciding factor. Without it, it was hard to see how a large force of bikers could be kept off the bridge. The bikes would come in quickly, even manage to pull off a surprise attack if they were smart and walked their bikes into close range. Small groups of defenders camped in the woods could be left out of the fight altogether, or arrive too late, or end up being caught in crossfires. A large group at the base of the bridge could be reinforced from town. That is, if the town wasn't too busy fighting off the attack from the north.

In the end, the committee agreed to Gil's request to set up a defense right at the bridge and to remain as a single force. Celine agreed as well, although she said she wanted to think about other options. William assured her that her strategic skills would come in handy no matter how they chose to organize.

Chapter 19

1

IT WAS CELINE'S new brainchild, so Celine had the honor of supervising construction of the defense. Help came from town, thirty more people, although they would be needed back in town as soon as construction was completed. William's only role appeared to be answering questions on Celine's behalf while she went about her business.

"Why are we building a fucking fort way out here?"

"Well, look back toward shore," William said, pointing. "This is a quarter-mile long, fifty-feet wide peninsula all the way from shore to bridge. From behind a stone wall we can shoot anything coming this way. Our flanks are protected on both sides by deep water. And we can be easily reinforced from town."

"But that's only a quarter mile. They can shoot us at that range, they don't have to charge at us."

"That's the reason for the stone wall."

"But can't they shoot down any reinforcements coming across the bridge?"

"Those are concrete railings lining the bridge. Six inches thick."

"We could be pinned down here for days."

"Who's going to have who pinned down? They will be stuck out there in the woods, fifty miles from Branson, sleeping on cold ground. We're bringing in mattresses and propane stoves as we speak."

"Forts never work."

"Of course they work. Why do you think they were built for thousands of years?"

The workers carried stone blocks the size of basketballs from the bridge footings and shoreline onto the top of the peninsula and stacked them two-deep. When finished, the wall would stand six feet high and thirty feet wide, crossing the road, and would extend ten feet back on each side, leaving the rear open to the bridge some twenty feet further back. "Stonehenge II," someone named it. Small notches were being left between rocks along the top row of stones to serve as shooting ports. Stones were set below the ports for shooters to stand on.

"Forts work," became the slogan for the project.

2

A long day of heavy labor completed the fort and the accessories which, in addition to mattresses, included various food containers, tarps in case of rain, medicine and bandage kits, water jugs, ammo boxes, night-vision goggles, toothbrushes and paste, and flags for signaling the town. Also set up were trip-wire alarms in case attackers tried to advance on the fort under cover of darkness.

All members of Camp Twain, old and new, fit comfortably behind the wall. The lone exception was Kat, whom William had sent into town with Riley and with instructions to stay at the church and assist Gil in any way that he needed her. Of course, she objected at first, but the promise of cold Coke and potato chips and some new clothes swung the deal.

For William, that night on the mattress under a clear sky with cool air off the lake was one to remember, in that low-key sort of way. Tom had brought news from Gil that Ellen had agreed to use her people to attack from the rear any biker assaults on the north side of the town. Gil expected the main assault would come on that side, where the town had no advantage of a bottleneck, but instead was wide open across a 180-degree front. While he rested, William imagined in countless scenarios what that kind of action would be like for Ellen, a woman in her sixties trying to manage a battle of that size. He hoped a guy like Herc would be of some use to her in that situation, but some people were not capable of being helpful in any situation. He felt profound concern for her, equal to what he felt for Kat. The cynicism of recent years had been replaced in his heart by a human connection, it seemed. He wanted all these people to come out of this okay. Some of them, he knew, were even Arkansans, a group he had been unfairly critical of. Hope for humanity. Really? Now? It seemed a newly discovered sensitivity, like it had risen from the earth or descended from the sky as a gift from somewhere, or other such poetic marvel.

Sleep hit him sometime around one o'clock and held him fast and peaceful until dawn, when the movements of others around him brought him back to the real world. As he ate a peanut butter sandwich for breakfast, he thought he heard the popping sound of distant gunfire muted by the heavy morning air.

3

Everyone had heard it. Only a few spoke of it. Many eyes looked to the town, where, here and there, figures moved along the edges of the main street, most heading north. The few remaining work reinforcements at the wall hurried back to town.

The sound quieted for at least an hour before picking up again. William tried to estimate the number of guns that would be involved but had no real basis for such an estimate. "This it?" he asked Celine as she passed by him from her mattress to one of the food containers.

"Not sure," she said. "Target practice is a possibility. Watch for the flag."

A red bedsheet hung from the highest point on the church was to be the signal. But no flag yet.

Other eyes were forward, toward the south span of highway and the woods on either side. Ears keened on the possibility of cycle noise. The rumble of twenty, thirty, fifty bikes? How much firepower would they throw at the skinny bunch of cowering twits trying to fort themselves against a pack of wolves?

Celine ran through some of the possibilities with her fighters. The gangs might send out a small detachment to probe the wall with a little fire to see what kind of response they would get and hold back their main force. They might go for a surprise attack in full force, relying on the speed of their bikes, probably with some kind of shielding in front, and hoping to scare off the defenders. They might try a night approach and lob Molotov cocktails over the wall, perhaps construct a primitive wood or metal wall of their own within easy range. The possibility of fire bombs clearly frightened some of the defenders. So much so that Celine immediately sent Tom back to town to get a couple of fire extinguishers. "We might want our own," William suggested. "Fire bombs, I mean." Celine sent another runner to see what could be had along those lines.

Three more times that day the gunfire could be heard north of the town, and when Tom returned with the fire extinguishers, he confirmed that it was the real thing, but not the "big thing." The gangs were trying to see what kind of answer they would get, was all, like Celine had suggested. But behind the shooting, the sound of what could be a hundred bikes, Tom said, was downright frightening to the town.

The final event of the day, at dusk, was the arrival of the makings of twenty-four fire bombs: a four-gallon plastic tank of gasoline, a case of empty beer bottles of various brands, and rags.

Chapter 20

1

DURING THE NIGHT they were all awakened by the slow rise of bike thunder from the hills to the south. The gangs were clearly not trying to hide their approach. It seemed to William to be a deliberate show aimed to intimidate, as they revved and growled and rode in as close as possible without exposing themselves to gunfire. He assumed they had seen the fort and knew not to attempt any kind of charge down a stretch of narrow, open road. When the show finally died down, the occupants of the fort trained all eyes on the dark hillside and woods.

"No. No," Celine said, pulling two of the men down from the crest of the wall. "If they see anything that looks like a head on this wall, they will punch a hole in it."

Others dropped into full cover as well.

"Let them sport with us for a while. They won't get serious right away," Celine said.

When dawn light began to creep in, Celine showed the defenders how to keep watch. At the end of each short sidewall she had placed four rocks at ninety-degree angles to the sidewalls, stacked in a two-by-two square arrangement. A small hole was left in the center of the arrangement to provide a view down the road. The observers were to lie behind the mini-walls and stay hidden. They didn't want to draw fire at those positions. Defenders would take turns and let the others know if they saw any movement toward the fort.

"I want everyone to stay off the gun ports unless it's absolutely necessary to rise up and shoot," Celine said. "Rely on our spotters. We're in no danger unless they come at us."

2

Small flakes off the crest of the wall began to fly about an hour after sunrise. The metallic "chink" sounds of bullets on stone were followed half a second later by the distant pops of the rifles. All defenders but the spotters sat in silence with their backs against the wall. Two smoked precious cigarettes, a few ate, but most just waited with their thoughts. Meanwhile, shooting could also be heard in town again, and at a new level of intensity.

Two hours of "sport" was followed by something that sounded more serious. The bikes had been mostly quiet, but the growl of a bigger engine, coming down the hill, caught everyone's attention.

"What do you see?" was the question being asked repeatedly of the spotters. "Nothing yet," was always the answer. The big growl only got bigger; whatever it was, closer. A screeching or rasping sound accompanied the sound of the engine.

Then, "I see something," came from Amanda, one of the spotters.

"Yep, me too," said Tom, the other spotter.

Celine hurried over to Tom's position and changed places with him to have her own look.

"Put some gas into a few of those bottles," Celine said. "Stopper them with rags. William, you got a lighter?"

William pulled his lighter from his pants pocket. "I do."

Kevin and Robert filled and stoppered the bottles. The approaching machine, whatever it was, seemed to be getting close to the foot of the peninsula.

"All I see is a big plate of metal," Amanda said.

"There's a truck behind it," Celine added. "I can see the back end of its bed. A big pickup, I think."

"Sounds like they've put together a moving screen," William said, without looking. "Can you see under it?"

"There is no under," said Celine. "Its scraping bottom on the pavement. Sparks everywhere."

"Must be shooters hiding behind it," said William. "Or those firebombers you were worried about."

The beast kept coming, growing only louder.

"Took a lot of gas to get that thing here from Branson," Robert said.

"We can't let it get close!" Celine yelled. "Who can throw good?"

The defenders looked around at each other for a moment.

"I was a pitcher in baseball," Tom said. "I can throw one of those things forty yards, I'll bet."

"Get it high over the top of the screen," said William. "There's a truck behind it. You want to hit the truck."

Rifle fire then started hitting the wall.

"They're shooting blindly from behind that thing," Celine said. "Keep your heads down. Hammer, you and Sam get on the fire extinguishers."

Staying low, Sam picked one up nearby. "I don't know how to use it," she said. Hammer scurried over and showed her, then picked up the other.

"A hundred yards, now!" said Celine.

"I'd say seventy," said Amanda. "I played rugby."

"Seventy!" said Celine.

"Tell me when it's forty!" William yelled, lighter at the ready. He moved into position beside Tom who held one of the full bottles.

3

You're going to have to take a quick look," William told Tom. "To gauge the distance."

"I know."

"Fifty!" yelled Celine.

The beast sounded like it was almost on top of them. Bullets pounded the wall indiscriminately, top to bottom.

"How do they drive that thing if they can't see!" someone shouted.

"The white lines," William answered. Not that it mattered.

"Forty!"

Tom held the bottle out for William. William struck the lighter and touched the flame to the rag.

Tom grabbed his quick look, then drew back his arm and hand. The flame flashed forward, and up went the bomb. William watched it sail high then drop out of sight behind the top of the stone wall. He heard the "whoosh" of the explosion.

"Hit the shield!" Celine yelled. "Next one."

William lit and Tom threw again.

Whoosh!

"Top of the shield! Fuck!"

Screams came from beyond the wall.

"Shoot!" yelled Celine.

All but Tom, William, and the spotters raised up and fired over the wall at whatever it was they saw out there.

"Throw another!" from Celine.

Bomb away, another explosion. More screams from the beast.

Now William could hear the roar of the fire. The truck's engine seemed to have quit.

"They're running for it!" Robert yelled. "Fuckers!" He fired his weapon with a rage in his eyes.

"Fucking ball of fire!" Celine yelled. "You got the truck!"

Sam ducked behind the wall next to where William stood. "Everyone down!" she screamed.

4

The fire raged for ten minutes before slowly fading out. Meanwhile, bullets continued to strike the wall as all defenders sat patiently behind it, some with smiles on their faces, others with lingering signs of fear, no one wounded yet.

"They were burning alive," Sharonne said, her face ghostly white and sweaty.

"I put two of them out of their misery," said Robert.

"One made it to the water," said Hammer. "But he sank."

"That truck's blocking my view some," said Amanda, still lying in her spotter position.

"Not sure we can do anything about that," Celine said, returning from her own spotting position. She waved Joe over to replace her there.

"Could serve as a great symbol of discouragement to the gangs," William offered.

"Psychological warfare," said Sam.

They ate, drank, talked in small groups. The bullets eventually stopped arriving, as the shooters must have finally realized that they were wasting ammunition.

"Thank God it wasn't us who got firebombed," Sam said. "I don't know if the extinguishers would be enough."

"Hope we don't have to find out," said William. "All in all, I think we are in a great position here. I'm not so sure about Kimberling."

The shooting in town was off-and-on but intense when on. The red flag flew atop the church, someone finally noticed: a warning that was almost laughable in comparison to the earlier thunder of motorcycles on the hills and the barrage of bullets coming their way.

"You look worried, William," Sam said.

William laughed. "Who doesn't?"

Sam then laughed as well. "Oh, yeah. What I meant was that something might be on your mind other than the obvious."

"Oh, a friend of mine, Ellen, is up there north of Kimberling, probably in her own fight. Just worried about her."

"Oh, really? A friend, huh?" Sam said with a wry smile.

"Okay. A very good friend." He shoved Sam playfully on the shoulder. "My guess is that it's worse there than here. Celine really nailed it, didn't she?"

Sam glanced at Celine, who was talking with Hammer and Amanda on the far side of the fort. "Shish, she'll hear you and grow a big head."

Celine pulled a piece of blue cloth from a bag and tied it to the end of her rifle. She searched for a good line of sight toward town, then waved it high.

"Our sign that we are holding the bridge," said Sam.

5

The bridge, the peninsula, the hills and woods, even the town were quiet all afternoon except for an occasional bullet striking the stone wall or flying overhead. The defenders assumed their enemy was planning a new approach, a new attack of some kind. No one could imagine what form that might take that would have any chance of success, unless they were bringing in artillery. Joe suggested a catapult heaving fireballs of tar and asphalt. "Not as easy as it sounds," William replied. "It takes considerable fine-tuning to get any accuracy at that distance. I doubt they have the engineers."

Just before dusk, the roar of engines suddenly broke the calm and cascaded down the hill. A lot of engines— their roar building, then fading as it seemed they were retreating to the south.

"Some kind of trick," Robert suggested.

No one doubted it.

When the sound had completely dissipated, followed by half an hour of silence, some began to wonder.

"Would they give up that easy?" Amanda asked no one in particular.

"I think they may have taken their best shot," Celine said. "And run into a stone wall."

Lots of laughter.

"Anyone have a guess as to how many were out there?" William asked. "Hammer, the sound of the bikes tell you anything?"

Hammer shrugged. "If I had to guess, I would say twenty or twenty-five. Some might be riding double, to save on gas."

"That's a lot of reinforcement for the attack on the town," William said. "If that's where they're going."

No one cared to offer an opinion on that.

"Well, we've got to stay here," Celine finally said. "Some of them could still be out there, and the others might come back."

"How do we test for a trick?" William asked.

"Poke your head up, William," Jim said, smiling.

William chuckled. "Yeah, there's that. Bullets would probably bounce right off, like these rocks."

"Well, it's almost dark," said Sam. "Nothing we can do but wait."

6

A few hours after dark, a messenger arrived from town, having crossed the bridge with no shots fired. He reported to Celine. William listened in.

"We think they are getting reinforcements," he said. "A lot of bikes came in on the upper highway. Gil says to tell William that the help from Ellen's people hasn't showed up."

Celine looked at William. "Is that possible?"

"Shit," said William. He looked to the town, which was still quiet. "Something must have gone wrong."

"Gil wants to know if you can come over and help him figure a way to get word to Ellen," the messenger said to William.

William thought for a moment. "Christ, if Gil doesn't know...."

No one moved or spoke, they just stared at William.

William waved Hammer in close. "Did you ever get that bike fixed?" he asked.

"You mean the one with the shot-up gas tank?"

"Yeah, that one."

"Sure. I found the abandoned bikes right where you said. I took a good tank off one of those and put it on the other."

"You carried it that far?"

"Wasn't very far, really. Even when I had it full."

"So, the good bike is still there with the others we shot up?"

"Yep. I put it back on the heap with the others. Covered them over nice."

"You got the key?"

"Key is in it."

William stood up and grabbed his rifle and walked over to the bag of flags, He pulled out a piece of white cloth and tied it to the end of his rifle. "I don't want anyone talking me out of this," he said as he wrapped the cloth tightly around the barrel.

He walked to the side of the wall, slid around the spotting nook and along the outside of the wall, then hurried to the metal shield still attached to the truck. Along the way he heard someone from behind the wall say, "Is he nuts?"

Once at the shield, William unfurled the cloth and moved it subtly about the edges of the shield where, even in the dark, a white cloth would be dimly visible from the hill.

"You know what you're doing?" Celine barked in his direction.

He stood then and walked past the remains of the pickup, holding the flag out to his side where, he hoped, any shots would be directed.

No shots.

He tripped over something and spied a darker shade at his feet—the shape of a body. He felt with his hands and found a leather jacket which he stripped from the body. Then a helmet.

Jacket and helmet, now worn by William. He stepped into a trot, heading directly down the peninsula.

He *was* nuts. No doubt about it. It was the only explanation as to why he didn't seem to give a shit. Images of Ellen popped into his mind. Maybe that was it.

He reached the foot of the peninsula and the woods without incident. Either they were gone, or they were all asleep, or someone saw him and took him for one of their own. He stripped the flag off his rifle and slung the rifle over his shoulder and began the long uphill hike. The whole area smelled of burnt gunpowder.

Chapter 21

1

HALF AN HOUR BEFORE dawn William began his search for the bike stash. Two hours later, he found it. He had the bike on the road minutes after that, getting the feel for a machine the likes of which he hadn't rode for almost twenty years. The clutch gave him the most trouble, missed gears almost throwing him out of the seat. Brakes seemed touchy. The damn helmet didn't fit well and kept sliding over his eyes. He had to ditch it.

He had looked at the maps often enough to know the route south to Highway 86, then west to 39 and north to the next bridge over the lake. After the bridge, he would continue north to 76 and back east to 13. Then Highway 13 south to whatever county road could get him close to Ellen's compound. A long way around but the only way, other than through the Branson area. If any of the bad guys might see through his faint disguise, it would be in Branson.

A long way around. He could run into another biker at any point. Hopefully, they were all busy shooting up Kimberling City.

2

Traveling east on Highway 76, William passed through another wrecked town, this one called Cape Fair, and soon after came to a small bridge over a river. As he approached the bridge, a man with a gun walked out of the shade at the side of the road. Not wanting to be shot in the back, William decided he should stop when the man waved him down.

"What you doing way up here, man?" the guy said. "The party's down in Kimberling."

"Heading there now."

"Right. Where from?"

William pointed south. "Down by Lampe. We had trouble at the bridge there."

The man laughed. "Yeah, them others that came through told me about that. You kill any of them bastards?"

"Don't know. Threw a lot of lead at them."

"Hah. Wished I coulda seen that."

"How come you're way up here? Need a ride?"

"Oh, hell, no. This here's my job. Us here in Reeds, we don't have bikes. You outta Branson?"

"No. Lampe."

"Oh, yeah, I heard of you guys."

"You're outta Reeds Spring, then?"

"Yep. We work for them in Branson. Pays pretty good, if you like eating dog food." He laughed.

"You know Linda Gordon?"

"Why, hell yeah. Boss lady."

"I hear she runs a tight ship."

"Tight at both ends, mister." He laughed again. "Nothing goes in, nothing comes out."

"I hear the Branson people talk about her. Not nice things, mostly."

He shook his head. "Nah, they don't like her, but she does for them good, I guess." He drew fingers across his throat. "Like that."

"Dirty work?"

"All kinda dirty work around here. She does her share."

William nodded. "I gotta get going. Okay with you?"

He waved William on, laughed. "Don't catch no bullet, now."

3

With only his mental map to guide him, William had only a rough idea of the location of Ellen's compound, along with his recollection of natural markers. He decided to avoid Highway 13 altogether and turned south on a gravel road that, by his estimation, was close to due north of the compound. He remembered an east-west gravel where Ellen led him off the trail on foot. There was the long driveway to the compound, which broke from another, very narrow dirt road.

He simply bore south until encountering an east-west crossing, took that one west for a few miles, gave it up and turned back to try the east branch. But no luck that way, either. He resumed heading south on the first road.

A mile on, another crossing road veered southwest around a turn. That one dead-ended at a steep ravine half a mile in, at a small cluster of trailer homes. The northeast branch wound along a dry creek bed for a couple of miles before crossing yet another southbound gravel. He tried that one.

Not far along, he crossed a low-water bridge over another dry creek. Just past the bridge, he found a skinny dirt road skittering under heavy oak branches. It had the look of a private drive but offered no signs. He rode another half mile on the gravel until he saw what he was hoping for: a large mulberry tree with a bark notch. He parked the bike in nearby brush, unshouldered his rifle, and started down the little path that he and Ellen had followed to the compound.

4

He expected to encounter a lookout somewhere near the gate. He even waited there for a time, considering the best approach. If Ellen was still in charge, there would be no problem. If not....

He opted for the woods, a dense thicket of young trees cut by numerous *ad hoc* trails used by the compound's hunters. When he came upon the first outbuilding, a storage shed, he hunkered down, out of sight from the big house. Over the course of half an hour he heard voices in various directions but saw little, his field of view being too narrow. He backed deeper into the woods and moved in a blind arc to where he guessed Ellen's shelter would be. He came close; he could see her place, and he couldn't miss the large-bodied, bearded Cal sitting outside the door with a gun in his hands.

William shucked his rifle, made his way to the top of the shelter, and crawled over the grassy roof to the spot above the door.

"Cal," William said.

Cal jumped and looked up.

"You need to go get Herc," said William. "I need to talk to him."

Cal froze for a moment. "Herc? Why? What are you doing here?"

"I'll explain that when he gets here."

Cal looked to the door.

"Is she okay?" William asked.

"Yeah. Pretty good."

"Treated okay?"

Cal shrugged a little. "He hit her once. He beat Emmitt pretty bad."

"Emmitt's here?"

"Yeah, inside with Ellen."

"Can you get Herc, then?"

Cal seemed a bit reluctant but finally started to move. "I guess."

William sat atop the roof and waited, feet dangling over the roof's edge and directly above the door. He pulled his pistol and set it behind him on the grassy roof.

5

Herc arrived with two of his supporters, Bruce and another whose name William had forgotten. All had surprised looks on their faces. Cal brought up the rear. Behind them, at the front of the big house, several of the others stood watching.

"What the fuck do you want?" Herc asked as he came to a stop ten feet from Ellen's door.

"Well, I'd like you to release Ellen, for one. And Emmitt. But I also want you to change your mind on the business of helping out with Kimberling City."

"How in the hell did you even get here? And what makes you think we care what you want?"

"Wasn't easy getting here, I'll say that. I think it's in your best interest to do the right thing and follow through on your agreement with Kimberling City."

"I have no agreement. That was Ellen's doing and it's bullshit."

"What happens to you and the others here if the gangs knock out Kimberling? You think they are going to leave you alone then?"

"Why wouldn't they?"

"Because that's not what they do. They will ride in here and take whatever you have and hang your bodies from trees."

"I don't see it that way."

"You're more afraid of a fight than certain annihilation?"

Herc pulled his rifle from his shoulder and raised the barrel toward William. "I could plunk you right off your little perch and be done with this. End of story."

"He does have a point," Cal said, causing Herc to turn his head.

"We've settled this," Herc said. He turned back to William. "This old crapbag has shit for brains. That's about it."

Cal's girlfriend, Sean, came running from the direction of the big house. "Jesus, Herc!" she shouted. "Be sensible if you possibly can!" She slowed beside her husband and led him by the arm to join Herc and the other two. "I met those people down there, Herc. I doctored their wounded. They are good people and we should be on their side."

Herc glared at her. "I'm not going over this again. Get it through your thick skull. Question me again and I'll lock you away on restricted rations."

Cal stepped between those two and frowned at Herc. "That's going too far, Herc."

The shelter door then opened with a creak. Ellen and Emmitt stepped out.

"I think everyone here understands this but you, Herc," Ellen said. "Maybe even you do, but something is keeping you from doing the right thing." Ellen looked up and saw William and offered him a slim smile.

"What the fuck is this?" said Herc. "I'm the one making the calls here."

"Only because you have all the guns," said Ellen.

"Not all the guns," Emmitt said. "You missed one," he said to Herc. His hand circled from around his back, holding a pistol. He pointed the gun, fired two shots in quick succession, both striking Herc in the chest. Herc dropped instantly to the ground and suddenly lay coldly quiet in the bright sun.

"That's one for Kimberling and one for me," Emmitt said.

6

"The time had come," Emmitt explained to the group, after they had disposed of the body and gathered at the big house. Emmitt's face was plastered with bruises and minor cuts and band-aids.

"My god, that was extreme," Sean told him, still appearing somewhat shaken.

"You can hang me for it, if you want," said Emmitt. "Doesn't really matter to me. I was going to kill that bastard sooner or later."

"Why?" Sean asked.

"Kimberling is reason enough. He's also responsible for the death of my daughter."

Everyone was quiet.

"Say more," William finally said.

Emmitt hesitated, appeared to be trying to collect himself emotionally. "I lived in Rolla before all this...shit broke out. I knew Herc there. We were both retired military. I knew him from veteran's events. When it came time to get out of that town, a friend of his offered my daughter and I, and Herc, rides to the Reeds Spring compound. On the way, at a Quick-Stop, I went to use the restroom. When I came out, Herc and his buddy were gone, my daughter with them. She was nineteen."

"Jesus," said Sean.

"Oh, no," Jan the cook said.

"I walked to Reeds Spring. Took me almost a week. When I got there, she was..." he struggled to get the word out, "...dead. When he saw me, Herc disappeared. His friend told me about what happened, and where Herc was headed, before I shot him."

William noticed how most heads were bowed in listening to this.

"So, all this time here, Herc knew you were out to get him?" William asked.

Emmitt shrugged. "I suppose he wasn't sure what I knew, what his friend had told me, but I'm sure he was

271

suspicious. He kept a close eye on me. When I confronted him, he claimed that his friend had been responsible for the abduction, that another car had pulled up to the Quick -Stop with some rough-looking people in it who threatened them, so they took off. Herc said he told his friend to go back, but his friend refused. All bullshit, of course."

"You asked him about your daughter?"

"Oh, neither of them knew anything about what happened to her, except that her body was found in the woods. Herc had the fucking gall to apologize on behalf of his friend."

7

"It was my pistol," Ellen said, when she and William sat under the maple at evening planning the move against the gangs at Kimberling. "I had showed him where I hid it, but I didn't think he had any intention of using it unless they came to do us harm."

"I believe they intended to do you harm," William said.

"Well, yes, they intended to harm all of us, directly or indirectly.

"I won't have Bruce and John with us," she said of Herc's main supporters. "Whatever we decide to do."

"Send them on their way?"

"Yes."

"Two fewer guns."

"I don't care. Others will have to stay here with the kids."

"I think we need to move tonight," William said. "Get close by morning, then listen for the shooting and come in behind them."

She nodded. "You a military tactician now?"

He laughed. "Just carrying out orders. That's just part of the master plan. Gil's plan."

"I see." She shifted in close to William and hugged him. "You have no idea how happy I was to see you sitting on my roof today. Even in the middle of all that. How long were you up there?"

"Oh, well, for days. Just waiting for the right moment to surprise you."

Chapter 22

1

ONLY EIGHT OF THEM made the trip south, fewer than William and Ellen had hoped for, but the prospect of a shooting war was too much for some. They traveled at night, following the same route William had used before with Ellen and then with Emmitt. When they neared the town's northern edge, they heard no shooting. No bike noise. They decided to go into cover and wait for dawn. They chose a section of roof fallen slant-wise into the interior of a burned-out house, brick walls on two sides, darkly shaded beneath the roof.

The first light brought the sounds of a fight. All of it was to the east of where William and the others sat in cover, but close enough to place them almost where they needed to be.

"That sounds like it's probably on or nearly on the highway," Emmitt said.

"A street fight in the middle of town?" William asked.

"It's not Fallujah," Emmitt said. "It's a broad street with buildings somewhat scattered and well back from the highway. Probably clear lines of combat."

"Does that mean we can come in behind the bad guys?" Ellen asked.

"It's better for us, yes. Not much chance of getting mixed in among them. But we have to be very careful. Step by step, we have to know what we're getting into."

"So we stick together until we have the situation figured out, then spread ourselves around—or do we stay together?"

Emmitt didn't seem to have an answer for that.

"I suppose there are pros and cons either way," William said. "Why don't we wait and see what it looks like?"

"Do we shoot them in the back?" Sean asked.

Silence for a moment.

"That's war," said Emmitt. "If we ask them to turn around, then they shoot us."

"The idea here is not to give the impression that they are surrounded and convince them to pull out," said William. "We do that, and they will be back again tomorrow. The idea is to shoot as many as we can so they don't have the numbers to come back, but to do it stealthily, so they don't see where it's coming from."

Emmitt nodded.

"That's a hard thing to accept, I know," William said. "I've been thinking about such things for quite some time. Kill or be killed is not civilized. It's primitive and undesirable. But that's where we are right now."

"We pick them off?" said Ellen. "One here, one there? At a distance? We don't want to make a big show of it?"

"Exactly," said William.

"Then I think we should stick together," said Cal. "For protection. In case they do get wise to us and come at us."

Lots of nodding heads.

"Agreed, then," said Ellen. "Unless or until the situation calls for a change."

2

They left all their gear and supplies, except their weapons and ammunition, in their shelter and looped northward, staying well behind the shooting. When they reached the highway, they moved back toward town along the east side. They advanced one person at a time, from cover to cover, with all the speed each could muster, which, in William's case, wasn't much. He felt vulnerable in open daylight and would have preferred rain, fog, a Minnesota blizzard. Emmitt led each advance, something he insisted on. When he reached a small used car lot, Emmitt signaled them to wait and slipped between cars for a better view ahead. A short while later he reappeared and waved them forward.

Emmitt pointed at the last row of cars when William and the others joined him. "Good view from there," he said. Most of the cars had been stripped of anything useful, doors and hoods left open.

"What are we looking at?" William asked.

"Lots of targets, just down the hill, about a hundred to two hundred yards." Emmitt pointed to the left. "There's a bunch sitting behind a hairdresser place, six or seven. Looks like they're taking a break. Others are spread around, shooting at targets farther down the hill. Backs to us."

William eyed each member of their little squad in turn. Nerves were on edge at every stop.

"Everyone know how to use their rifle?" he asked.

"They do," Ellen replied. "I made them learn."

"We need to hit that group of six," William said. "Each of us will select a target in turn, then we shoot together. Rifles on semi."

They moved forward to the spot Emmitt had picked. He directed each person to a position behind two adjacent cars. The scene Emmitt described lay before them. The target group was six male bikers, standing and talking, several smoking.

"Won't the others farther down hear us shooting, and see us?" Sean asked.

"I don't know," said William. "If we shoot at the others, someone in that group, though, is bound to. Those further down are making plenty of their own noise."

Ellen nodded. "If we are spotted, we run back, all the way back to where we stored our packs and wait for things to cool down."

"Seems like a plan," said Cal. "Let's shoot the fucks."

"Okay," William said. "I will take the one furthest left in that group. I'll shoot first, two shots, then everyone else come in. Two shots each. Who you got, Cal?"

"The next in line from the left."

When all but Jan and Sean had picked their targets, William told those two to have rifles ready and pointed, but not to shoot unless someone missed. "Hold steady, everyone. Accuracy is most important. It's a little downhill, so aim at their belts. Safeties off."

3

Five were down when Sean and Jan took their shots and brought down the sixth.

"Now duck!" William said as he dipped behind the car. The others followed.

"Shit, I missed," said Cal.

"Jan got him," said Ellen.

William peeked around the back end of the car for a view farther down the hill.

"Any problem?" Ellen asked.

"They don't seem to have noticed."

The shooting below continued at a frantic pace. William took another look to confirm no one there had suspicions.

"Let's give it minute," said Emmitt. He looked again toward the hairdresser shop. "Fuck. One of them is still moving. Shit, now he's gone."

"What?" Ellen asked.

"One of the bunch we shot. He limped off, behind the building."

Emmitt dropped his rifle and pulled his pistol and darted into the open and down toward where the bodies lay.

"Oh, no," said Sean.

4

All the gunfire from the line of bikers lower down the hillside did not mask the rapid exchange of shots from behind the hairdresser's. William and the others waited and watched. "Shit," Cal grumbled. "I missed him."

They waited some more. Cal began to move toward the front of the car and William could see his purpose on his face. He grabbed Cal by the shirt and pulled him back and onto the ground. "No," William said. "Not you."

"Cal, no way," Sean pleaded as she threw her body over his legs.

William looked down at the hairdresser shop, saw nothing but the bodies, then again at the gang's line of shooters. No one there had a clue, he decided. He slid away from the car and hurried toward the shop, across a patch of gravel driveway, and beneath a lone, sprawling oak tree, and past the dead men lying where they had been shot, all the way to the corner of the building. Rifle at the front, he spun around the corner.

Two men lay on the shaded grass of the back lawn, not ten feet apart.

Emmitt was dead. Shot in the forehead. The other man was also dead. It appeared Emmitt had shot him in the chest at least twice. Not square enough to kill him outright, it seemed.

"Shit," William said. He took a moment to collect himself, then bent down and patted Emmitt on the shoulder. "So sorry, Emmitt." In a useless gesture, he straightened the man's shirt collar. "Thanks, man." He cursed under his breath again, then he pulled away and hurried back to the car lot.

5

"This killing," Ellen said. "I feel like I'd almost rather die than do this." She sat with her back to the car door, her rifle in her lap, tears collecting in her eyes.

William nodded. He leaned in and kissed her on the head. "I know."

The gunfire from below never ceased. It had become a background noise that could almost be ignored.

"This is really the big attack, isn't it?" said Cal. "The one Emmitt talked about."

William looked at all their faces. Jan and George, so tense and out of place they rarely spoke. They were going through the motions in some semi-conscious state and were better off for it. Like Ellen, Sean could hardly bear the inhumanity, while Cal went about his business with some desperation, wanting to succeed to prove himself, perhaps to his girlfriend. Terry hadn't said a word since they left the compound, and not much before. William had concluded some time back that Terry was mentally disabled in some way and simply wanted to be told what to do.

"Yeah," William said. "This is the big one. We don't know what's going on in the rest of the world, but in our world, this is it. We do this, or we accept the end for ourselves. Like Ellen says, the distance between the two isn't that far."

"So, then, you want to quit?" Cal asked.

William shook his head. "I made up my mind on this many days ago. Good people are being killed. The bad guys have been winning. I want that to stop."

Cal nodded vigorously. "I don't even see them as people anymore," he said.

Ellen moaned. "That's not easy for me, Cal." She put a sunburned hand on his arm. "I know what we have to do. I just hate doing it. I just want someone—all of you, I guess—to know that."

William hugged her. Sean, then Jan, did the same.

6

From that point, William would do all the shooting, poor aim or not. Cal wanted to help, but his girlfriend asked him not to. William asked the others only to be on guard and watch their flanks for any movement that might signal something.

William put down six more bikers before he saw one of them pointing in his direction. Others began looking his way, and only moments later, four ran toward his flanks, two on each side.

"We have to go," William said to his crew. "Right now!"

In seconds everyone was on their feet, dodging through the rows of cars, then heading back to the north, directly away from the fighting, William leading.

"What is it?" Ellen asked.

"They spotted us. We're fine if we can keep out of sight."

They made it back across the highway and ran around burned houses, through overgrown lawns, and across empty residential drives cluttered with dead automobiles. William turned them westward back along the loop they had followed earlier and toward their shelter. He heard a scream and the distant pop of a rifle behind him.

William stopped and looked back. Sean lay on the ground, motionless, her rifle beside her, Cal bending over her. "Shit," William said, running past the others and back to Sean. He fired blindly into the assortment of blackened structures and empty lots and trees to the south. "God, no," he heard Ellen say.

Sean was out. Not breathing. Bleeding from her back. Cal seemed frozen in disbelief.

"Bring her," William said as he lifted her by the armpits. Cal took her feet and they carried her behind the wall of a garage with no roof. Two more shots followed, searing overhead. They crowded together behind the wall.

"Sean?" Cal said. He lifted her head, shook her shoulder. "Sean!" A huge hole lay open and pouring blood from Sean's upper abdomen.

Cal seemed to realize she wasn't breathing and began doing chest compressions. "Sean! Fuck!"

A couple of rounds smacked against the corner of the garage.

"She's gone," Ellen said, touching Cal on his back. "We have to go."

"Fuck that!" said Cal. He picked up the rifle he had dropped and stood up and fired around the corner. "Fuck you assholes!"

William stood up and pulled Cal back behind the wall. "She is dead, Cal," he said. "I'm sorry. We have to get out of here."

"I ain't leaving her," Cal said, pushing William away with a hand. "You guys beat it."

"Please, Cal," said Ellen.

"Go, then, fuckers! Everybody go! I'm going to kill those bastards!" He reached around the corner and fired again.

William grabbed Cal by the shirt and turned him and shook him hard. "Cal! Listen! Let's go. We'll come back for her."

"Fuck you will. Just go. I'm staying and that's it." He shoved William backwards and onto the ground.

Ellen helped William to his feet. "Let's go, William." She pulled him away and led him quickly into a small grove of trees behind a former house, the others following, except Cal. "We can't debate it or wait him out," she said. She kept moving.

7

They heard shooting behind them as they made their way to their shelter. Everyone looked back with frequency, with no way to be sure they weren't seen other than the absence of gunfire in their direction.

Once in the shelter, they were all breathing hard, especially George, who, with his large belly, seemed out of shape for this kind of thing.

"You okay, George?" William asked as he sat down with the others.

George nodded. "Yeah. Heart's a little fast, is all."

"Mine too," said William.

Ellen put her face in her hands and began sobbing. William scooted over to her and put his arm around her.

"I can't do this anymore," said Jan.

William looked at Jan, a question in his eyes.

Jan put her gun down. "I can't do this anymore." She wrapped her knees in her arms and laid her head on top of them.

"You okay, Terry?" William asked.

Terry shrugged. "Yeah." His hands and rifle were shaking slightly.

William bent around the collapsed section of roof and looked for pursuers.

"I don't see anyone," he told the others. He turned back to them. Ellen lifted her head.

"William," she said, "I am done, too. My God, it's my fault they were killed. I made them come."

William slid back beside her. "No. It's not. It's the circumstances. These gangs have done this, not you."

She shook her head. Tears streaked her smudged face. "I only know one thing. If I had not talked them into coming, they would be alive right now." She wiped at her eyes.

"Not for long. They fought for their survival. They lost, but they gave themselves a chance."

"I don't think I want any more chances. I won't kill for it." She laid her gun down.

William took her hand. "Do you mind if I fight for you?"

She looked him in the eye. She seemed to struggle for something to say but didn't find it.

"Well, I'm going to," he said. "With or without your approval."

8

A few hours later, William and Terry went out again. They made their way back to the highway north of town. The gunfire to the south was still in progress and loud enough to be close. Instead of returning to the car lot, they wormed their way carefully along an alley behind a small strip mall and found a two-foot high berm with a patch of trees from where they could see the activity down the hill. The backs of the bikers were in clear view—eleven that William counted. They shifted around a bit but were easy targets.

Terry tapped William on the shoulder and pointed to their right, into the weedy, tree-lined backyard of a demolished trailer. There was little yard to see, so many bikes were parked there.

"Time to get at it," William said quietly to Terry, as he trained his eyes back down the hill.

Terry tapped him on the shoulder again, pointed again. "That guy," he whispered.

William looked into the yard again and finally spotted the man smoking a cigarette under one of the trees, partially hidden by the array of bikes. A guard on those bikes. Of course.

William nodded to Terry and backed his head out of the way.

Terry raised his rifle alongside William's face and took aim. Pop.

The smoker slumped, cigarette falling from his lips in a cascade of sparks and into his lap, then tilted over onto his side.

They watched the yard for a few moments in case there were others, but nothing came of it.

William directed Terry's attention back down the hill. He raised his rifle. Terry did the same. Terry seemed to be waiting on William to start it. William found his first target and moved his finger onto the trigger.

The haunting words Ellen had uttered about not wanting to kill anymore turned his own stomach, an acutely unwanted visitation at that moment. He had been over and over this with himself, a hundred times. It was justifiable. On moral grounds, if human life and decency meant anything in the universe.

Justifiable, to get down into the gutter with the worst of people and do unto them as they would do. Not a betrayal of that decency. That's what justifiable meant. There was some aspect of decency itself that gave permission in extraordinary circumstances. It was not acceptance of the worst, it was defiance.

Terry lowered his rifle as he stared at William.

William then noticed that several of the bikers were not shooting below but were instead keeping watch on the uphill side. He lowered his own rifle, then his head down below the rim of the berm. Terry followed.

William looked over at the bikes. He estimated the number—twenty-five or thirty.

"This way," he said to Terry. He led him over into the yard, inspected the interior of what was left of the trailer to make sure it was unoccupied.

William then began moving bikes, crowding them into the center of the yard, piling them on top of one another and removing the caps from the gas tanks. Terry asked no questions and joined in.

9

William and Terry tipped some of the bikes atop the pile to spill the contents of their tanks. William then tore away a piece of the dead man's shirt and wrapped it around the end of an arm-sized stick he pulled from a dead tree branch. They spilled more gas over the pile. William soaked the torch with gas then stood back. He lit the rag and tossed it onto the middle of the heap, and instantly the fire burst high and wide. William stepped further back, pulling Terry with him. The exploding wave of heat roasted his face for a second.

Flames and black smoke shot into the sky. "No bikes, no gang," William muttered.

He led Terry back up the hill a short distance and into cover in a dense patch of trees and hedge.

"I do want to see this," William said as they watched the site of the burn. And within a few minutes, they began to arrive. Three or four, in a mild panic, looking hopelessly around for something to remedy what to them must have been an incomprehensible disaster. Then several more arrived. And more. Curses were audible from a hundred yards distant. Arms flailed through waves of heat.

Even greater panic set in as heads turned downhill and some of the bikers began running north. Some fell, and some then scattered in various directions. More fell, and William heard the gunfire that dropped them.

"Looks like Kimberling broke the line," William explained to Terry.

More bikers fell. Few turned to shoot back. They just ran. A moment later, the Kimberling fighters came charging into view, pursuing and shooting an enemy in desperate retreat. "Gotta love it," William said.

Chapter 23

1

ONCE THE LINE was broken, the Kimberling fighters had turned against the flanks of the remaining bikers and routed them as well. Seventy-two more bikes were captured, six more destroyed. The final body count on the gangs was sixty-three, with seven wounded and taken to the church for whatever care the Kimberling people wished to provide. Their chances were not good.

William and Terry had joined with the good guys for a time as they swept the town for more wounded and for any snipers that might be lingering. They then returned to their shelter and found Ellen and the others in fine condition, undetected and unharmed by retreating bikers.

"Thank God," Ellen said, hugging William. "It's over?"

He nodded. "Looks that way. I don't think you could say that's a viable gang any longer."

Ellen collapsed onto her rear and laid her arms over her knees. She looked up at him. "William, that was horrible. But I am so relieved."

He sat down beside her. "There are a lot of others feeling what you feel. People still alive, who wouldn't be." He put his arm around her. "I'd like you and Jan and the rest to come into town with me and see just how much relief there is there. It's like a fresh beginning."

"I'd like to see that."

"We burned their bikes," Terry said to Ellen as he came to stand over her.

"Their bikes?"

"That's right," William said. "Terry's the one who found them. I would say he rather ruined their day."

2

The town had lost eight of their own, including Ozark, with thirteen more wounded. So, there was no party at the church, but plenty of quiet, internal gratitude among the living. Some of that gratitude got expressed in words, much of it for William and Ellen and the rest of the "soldiers from the north."

"I just hope that's the end of it," was Ellen's frequent response as they stood with the crowd in the parking lot outside the church.

Gil sent out three burial squads with instructions to lay the dead bikers to rest well away from their own. A mass grave for them would be adequate. He asked for more mattresses to be brought into the nave for the wounded and for volunteers to administer antibiotics and painkillers and see that all bleeding was checked. He personally passed cold Cokes around to anyone who didn't refuse. Few refused. "Someday, maybe champagne," he said.

After checking in on the wounded again, Gil invited William into the office for a private conversation.

"I don't want the others to hear this, yet," Gil said, "but after you left the bridge, a guy came out of the woods down there. Said his name was Jim, and that he knew you and some of the others guarding the bridge."

William nodded. "Yeah, I know him."

"Well, this guy wanted to talk to me, but Celine told him we were busy over here and that she would take whatever he had to say. What he said was that he thought he had heard a helicopter the night before. He said it was a long way off, but that he had been in the Navy and knew helicopters. I told Celine to keep that to herself for now. False hope can be a downer."

William looked through the office window at the crowd in the parking lot. "Wouldn't that be something to add to this? Even beats a cold Coke."

3

The next thing William saw was the arched ceiling of the church nave emerging through a layer of semi-transparent film covering his eyes. Hushed voices surrounded him, half muted by the hum of the generator. He started to sit up, but a burning pain seized his back and abdomen and slammed him back down. Ellen's face appeared over him.

"William," she said. "William."

"What...what the hell?"

"Do you know where you are?" she asked.

"Huh? Yeah, in the church. What the hell happened?"

"You don't remember?"

"No. What the hell? I was talking to Gil about...something. Damn that hurts! Damn, what happened to me?"

"You went to help with the bridge, to help open it back up. Do you remember that?"

All this seemed unreal, some kind of hallucination. "No. Are you kidding?"

She put her hand on his chest. Tears in her eyes.

"You were shot, William," she said. "When you were over on the other side of the bridge, helping with the tear-down of the fort."

"Shot? By who?"

"A sniper. Celine went out and got him. Someone left behind after they pulled out."

"Holy shit. I don't remember any of that."

He touched the bandages wrapped around his waist. "How long have I been like this?"

"Not long. Only a few hours."

"My head feels like an explosion went off in there."

"They injected you with painkillers."

"Not doing much good, yet."

He tried to rise again but had to fall back. "Damn, that's something." He looked to each side and saw other mattresses and other wounded people. "How bad is it?"

Ellen struggled to answer. Her lips quivered. "The bullet hit you in the back and came out the front, just above your navel."

"Shit. That's not good."

Ellen began crying, sobbing. Her hands covered her face.

He reached up and took hold of her shoulder. He could feel the despair in her, flooding her.

"You know, don't you?" he said.

She looked at him, nodded, wiped at the tears on her face. She leaned down and embraced him, then laid her head alongside his.

Kat's face then came into view. Eyes and cheeks red, puffy. Mouth twisted. Her whole body shook.

"Kat. How are you, Kat?" he said.

She lowered to her knees and leaned in and grabbed his legs to steady herself. "I'm okay. They said you are shot." He could feel her hands trembling.

"Kat, that thing in Reeds Spring. It's not—"

"I don't care about that anymore. I'm staying with Sam and Robert. And-And with you."

He reached out and took one of her hands in his. "Oh, that's good, Kat. Really good."

"William? William, please don't die," Kat begged through a cascade of tears. "Please."

He smiled at her. "What makes you think I will?"

She pointed toward the entrance. "That's what they're saying."

"Well, what do they know?" he said. "Besides, the Seventh Cavalry is on its way."

Author

Jeffrey W. Tenney is retired and living in southwestern Missouri. He is a recipient of a Spur Award for fiction. In addition to writing novels, he occasionally writes stage plays and screenplays, and has produced two films, *The Raven's Prey* and *Heads*. He holds Masters degrees in Anthropology and Public Health.

CPSIA information can be obtained
at www.ICGtesting.com
Printed in the USA
BVHW031315070921
616233BV00013B/52